COMPANIONS OF
THE DARK

TEAM REAPER THRILLERS

Retribution

Deadly Intent

Termination Order

Blood Rush

Kill Count

Relentless

Lethal Tender

Empty Quiver

Barracuda!

Kill Theory

Danger Close

Global War

Fear The Reaper

Kane: Tooth & Nail

Kane: Center Mass

Kane: Darkness Upon Us

The Cabal

Collateral Damage

The Death Bringers

Hunting Ghosts

COMPANIONS OF THE DARK

A TEAM REAPER THRILLER

BRENT TOWNS

WOLFPACK
PUBLISHING
—— EST 2013 ——

Companions of the Dark
Paperback Edition
Copyright © 2024 Brent Towns

Wolfpack Publishing
701 S. Howard Ave. 106-324
Tampa, Florida 33609

wolfpackpublishing.com

Paperback ISBN 978-1-64734-078-0
eBook ISBN 978-1-64734-077-3
LCCN 2024933459

Thanks to Tony Park for the answers I had about the unknown.
Great author and lover of all things African.

TEAM REAPER

Command:
Mary Thurston
Luis Ferrero

Team Reaper:
John "Reaper" Kane
Cara Billings
Raymond "Knocker" Jensen
Les "Lofty" Travers
Richard "Brick" Peters

Bravo:
Pete Traynor
Pete Teller
Sam "Slick" Swift
Doctor Rosana Morales

COMPANIONS OF
THE DARK

PROLOGUE

"Falcon One-Zero to Bravo Zero-Two, over."

"Zero-Two reads you, Lima Charlie, Falcon, over," Kane replied from the ops room in Gaborone, Botswana.

"We're two mikes from the LZ, over."

"Copy."

Onboard the helicopter known as Falcon One-Zero was Strike Team Hyena, led by Ollie Richards. They were a four-man team now operating under the purview of Team Reaper. They were in Botswana trying to root out poachers who had stepped up their activity against a small and diminishing herd of elephants in Chobe National Park.

The rangers had reached out for help after one of their anti-poaching teams was massacred by the poachers responsible. But on further investigation, the poachers were discovered to be more than a little hi-tech.

Global got the call and they dispatched their team. Their new team.

Swift had picked up chatter that a team of poachers were working in the park that night and Hyena, along with a team from the anti-poaching squad had been dispatched to intercept them. Now they were only a couple of minutes out from their designated landing zone.

"Talk to me," Thurston said from behind Kane and Ferrero.

The former DEA agent said, "Hyena is two mikes out and on time. Bravo One, how are we looking on the LZ?"

"LZ looks clear, no heat signatures at this time," replied a female voice.

It was still hard to get used to not having Brooke in the pilot seat. The new Bravo One was Rani Perera, a Brit by birth with Sri Lankan parents. Before coming to Global she had flown Apache helicopters then crossing over to UAVs.

"Falcon One-Zero is one mike out."

Kane said, "Do another sweep, make sure, Rani."

"Roger, coming around for another sweep."

"What about the elephant herd?" Thurston asked.

"One klick to the east," Swift replied. "The satellite shows them bunched near a waterhole."

"No other heat signatures?"

"No, ma'am."

Kane suddenly felt nervous. Everything was going so smooth. Too smooth. Beside him, Ferrero said, "Relax, Reaper, they'll be on the ground in thirty seconds."

"Falcon One-Zero, flaring for landing."

"Oh, shit. Abort! Abort!" cried Rani. "Get out, now."

Suddenly the big screen came alive with heat signatures.

"What the hell?" Kane snapped. "Were they using some kind of cloaking material?"

In the background, Ferrero was talking on the radio. "Falcon One-Zero, abort. I say again, abort. The LZ is hot."

"Roger, Falcon One-Zero is aborting—oh, shit!"

Suddenly on the screen, the team back in ops saw the explosion that ripped through the helicopter. The comms went dead and what remained of the craft crashed onto the ground.

"Was that a missile or an RPG?" Kane barked.

No one answered.

"Missile or RPG?" he asked again, his voice harsher.

"Not sure at this time," Rani answered.

They all watched on as the heat signatures closed on the crash site.

Kane said, "Falcon One-Zero, copy?"

Static.

"Hyena One, copy?"

Static.

"Hyena Two, copy?"

Static.

"Hyena Three, copy?"

"They are all dead, American," an accented voice came back to ops. "Let this be a lesson to you. Stay out of Botswana. You do not belong here."

The line went dead.

Kane turned and stared at Ferrero. The former DEA man nodded. "All right, Reaper. Get them together."

PART ONE

THE FOG OF WAR

CHAPTER 1

Raymond "Knocker" Jensen dropped to a knee and scratched at his short beard, listening to the night sounds, and straining to hear anything unfamiliar or manmade. His partner for this patrol was former SAS Corporal Les "Lofty" Travers. The dark-haired man who stood around six-foot-one had been with the team for three weeks, taking the place of Axe who had been killed in Venezuela.

Travers was a good fit for the team, and because of his experience in Africa training the anti-poaching teams, even more so. This time it was different though. The anti-poaching team they were on patrol with were all young women, based on the Akashinga, the anti-poaching taskforce formed by a former Australian Commando.

Knocker waited for a moment and said into his comms. "Lofty, bring them up."

"Roger that."

A figure came out of the darkness and took up a position beside the Brit Kayla Moyo who was the anti-poaching team commander. She was in her late twenties, had short, scalp-hugging hair, skin the color of burnished copper, and a smile as white as the snow in midwinter. "What do you think?" she asked Knocker in her low tones.

"I don't know," he replied. "We can't be far from the river."

"Maybe two kilometers."

Of the elephant herds in Chobe, the small herd at the river was the one the poachers had targeted recently. Even though some of the elephants were adapting to years of hunting and being born without tusks, it wasn't happening fast enough. The ever more troubling part was the poachers were using cyanide to poison the water holes in Zimbabwe and killing everything that drank there. These were thought to be the same people who had allegedly wiped out Strike Team Hycna three weeks earlier, along with the anti-poaching team they were with.

In the aftermath of those events, John "Reaper" Kane, Team Reaper commander, had reached out to his people who had all been reassigned to other jobs. All but Cara had returned. She was still dealing with other issues and had said she wasn't ready to return. The team consisted of Kane, Richard "Brick" Peters, Knocker, and the new guy, Lofty Travers.

The poachers were coming across the border, killing the elephants, and then retreating. But elephants weren't their only targets. Recently there had been an uptick in the numbers of hippos being killed.

And anti-poaching squad members.

Movement behind them signaled the arrival of the

others. Travers joined them up front while the ten young women of the anti-poaching squad set up a small perimeter to the rear. Travers was about to speak when the deep-throated roar of a male lion rolled across the darkened landscape.

"He knows something is afoot," Kayla said softly. "We will have to be careful."

The longer Knocker spent with Kayla, the deeper his respect grew for her. The job that her people did was dangerous, but they never shirked their responsibility. Even when they came under fire or lost members; they were warriors to the last.

"Then we'd better stay off his menu," Knocker whispered.

"You will be safe," she said. "You are too scrawny for him to worry about."

Knocker grinned. "Bitch."

She returned his grin in the moonlight. "You wish."

"Lofty, take Suma and her girls and move around to your right until you reach the river. Once you get there, radio me for further instructions."

"Roger that."

Moments later, the big man from Liverpool disappeared into the darkness with the squad following along behind.

"Suma will keep him on his toes," Kayla said to Knocker. "I think she likes him."

"Great, that's all I need."

"Really?" she asked. "And you don't like me?"

"Can't bloody stand you," he replied.

"Liar."

"Bravo One, copy?" Knocker said, ignoring the jibe.

"Copy, Reaper Three," came the woman's voice over his comms.

"Rani, we're moving to the river. Lofty and his team are flanking around the right. so keep an eye out for them."

"Roger, Knocker. ISR is clear so far."

"Roger, out." He looked at Kayla. "Come on, let's move."

"Yes, boss."

————

MOSEKI CAMP

"All teams, hold position," Rani said in a low voice as though she might be overheard.

"Copy that."

"Copy your last. Holding position."

"What is it?" Luis Ferrero asked as he moved in behind his UAV team.

He was in his late forties, solidly built, with graying hair, although he'd swear it was a little grayer of late. Ferrero was second in command of the teams overall behind Mary Thurston and an experienced commander.

Rani said, "Pete, can you zoom in on the anomaly?"

Pete Teller, a former Master Sergeant in the US Air Force, was now the right-hand man in the UAV team. The big screen zoomed, and Ferrero wasn't sure what he was looking at.

"Someone talk to me before I go cross-eyed."

"At the center of the screen, on the other side of the river," Teller said. "Can you see the darkened area?"

"Christ, vaguely," Ferrero muttered.

"Get me a heat signature."

The feed changed and the object became clearer. "I

believe that the anomaly there could be our poachers," Rana said.

"Can you be sure?"

"Almost."

"Is that what happened to Hyena?"

"My guess would be no. Whoever ambushed Hyena was way more hi-tech."

"Great, just what we need." He stared at the screen. "Shit. Relay it to Knocker and Travers. I'll have a word with Mary. Just when we're about to move camps."

This was their last patrol before the new teams moved in. Reaper and the female anti-poaching squads were heading to a new location on the border with Zimbabwe where a new park was being set up to try and protect one of the largest elephant herds in Botswana. It was to be situated opposite Hwange National Park.

"What's happening?" John "Reaper" Kane asked as he entered the ops room.

He was a larger man, six-four, broad across the shoulders, and the team commander.

Ferrero said, "It would seem that our poachers are hiding in the grass."

"Ambush?"

"Maybe for the elephants. We've got Knocker and Lofty holding now until we work out what they're up to."

"What one would give for a Hellfire right now," Kane said.

"I agree," said Ferrero. "But as we know, that was one of the reasons why we were allowed to use UAVs in Botswana. Unarmed. Surveillance only. Now, does anyone have ideas?"

"What side are the elephants on?" Kane asked.

"They're on the same side as the teams approaching the river. Judging by their patterns over the past couple of weeks, they'll cross the water course."

"Is there any way Knocker and the others can turn them back?"

"There's no time for them to put themselves between the river and the herd," Rani replied.

"Then we need to find another way," Kane said.

"I have a way," Rani said. Then over the comms she continued, "Reaper Three and Four, make yourselves real small; things are about to get sketchy."

Kane stared at the UAV pilot and said, "What are you up to?"

She gave him a nervous smile. "You don't want to know."

———

CHOBE NATIONAL PARK, BOTSWANA

Knocker looked at Kayla and said, "What do you suppose she's up to?"

Kneeling beside him, she said, "How would I know something like that?"

"Bravo One, I need a sitrep, over," he said into his comms.

"Just keep this channel open, Reaper Three. Same with Reaper Four. Just in case."

"Just in case, what?"

Suddenly he heard it getting louder in the night air. Then it was there, flying no higher than thirty feet above the ground.

"Holy shit," Knocker yelped and hit the ground as

the UAV flew low over them. "Bravo One, what the fuck are you doing?"

"Hang on, Reaper Three. You're about to have visitors."

"What?"

Then the noise of the UAV was replaced by the rumbling of thunder. Then came the trumpeting. Knocker looked at Kayla and said, "You've got to be shitting me."

"Knocker, you have to move now," Rani said urgently over the comms. "Run east, I say again, run east."

Leaping to his feet he said, "Everyone on me."

As instructed, he headed east, followed by Kayla and the other women. Out of the darkness, shadows loomed, large, daunting. Their Synoprathetic suits might stop bullets, but there was no way in hell they would stop over 7,000 pounds of charging elephant.

As he ran, the long grass whipped around him. He could feel the vibrations through his feet. In his comms he heard Rani say, "Keep running, Reaper Three, you're almost clear."

"Fucking bollocks," he growled.

Then out of the gloom, a big bull elephant appeared. Almost 13,000 pounds of enraged beast who wanted to escape the manmade annoyance that had scared him and the rest of the herd.

"Jesus Christ!" Knocker exclaimed. He thought about bringing up his Heckler & Koch 417 to defend himself but reconsidered and kept running.

The whole team was armed with the larger stopping power of the 7.62 HK417. The anti-poaching squad, on the other hand, were all armed with the LWRC International, M6A2.

Eventually the trumpeting of the elephants grew quieter, more distant, as the gap between humans and beasts widened.

"Bravo One, what the fuck was that?" Knocker growled.

"That was me saving the elephants," she shot back at him. "Right at this point across the river you have a group of hi-tech poachers wearing some kind of cloaking material."

"Are they fucking Klingons or something?"

"Be advised, we've now lost them," Rani said.

"Did you say they were across the river?"

"Roger that."

"Proceeding to the river. Break. Lofty, you on channel?"

"Copy, Mucker."

"Move to the river and hold."

"Roger that."

The two teams pressed forward until they reached the water course. It was neither wide nor deep but supported a healthy population of Nile crocodiles. Whether they were there or upstream, no one knew, nor were they desirous to find out.

Kayla kneeled beside him back from the water's edge. "This is as far as we go."

"Unless you want to be first across," Knocker said.

"I would rather be first than second."

"Bravo One, sitrep, over."

"No sign, Reaper Three. Maybe—"

The night was ripped apart by gunfire, tracers cutting through the darkness.

"Son of a bitch," the Brit growled as he dove to the ground.

The long grass hid them well, but the bullets were

mowing the stalks down. Over his comms he heard Lofty say, "I can see muzzle flashes across the river. Assaulting forward."

"Damn it, Lofty, there's fucking crocs in that river."

"You just have to spoil everything, don't you," Lofty replied. "Just sit tight and we'll see what we can do."

"Reaper Four, hold position," Ferrero said over the comms channel. "Do not enter that water."

"Sorry, Zero, you're breaking up. Proceeding as planned."

Knocker shook his head as he hugged the ground. "Ballsy, Lofty old mate, bloody ballsy."

WHEN THE GUNFIRE lit up the night, Lofty knew there was only one course of action to take. With the other team pinned down he'd called Suma over to him. "Can we get across the river in one piece?"

"Maybe two of us. Not all. Old Kwena will see to that," she said using the Tswana word for crocodile.

"Then let's get about it."

Lofty edged toward the river and started across. The bottom was muddy, and he tried not to splash too much. The water level rose up his body until it was around his waist. Suma was right behind him while the other women from the anti-poaching squad covered their passage across.

The river was forty meters wide, and they were now halfway. If a crocodile came at them now, they were done. But nothing happened.

Tentative footstep after tentative footstep, the pair crossed the river. Luck was on their side. And when they emerged dripping wet on the far bank, Lofty breathed a sigh of relief. "I think you are blessed, white man," Suma said lightly.

"It must be the company I keep," he said and brought his 417 up to scan ahead of them. "It's all clear."

They moved toward the firing, keeping low through the long grass. The gunfire from across the river was growing more intense as Knocker had his squad returning fire as best they could.

"Reaper Three, copy?"

"Copy, Reaper Four."

"We're feet dry and closing on the shooters from the east."

"Copy, will adjust fire accordingly."

Lofty brought up his weapon and looked through the sights. He said to Suma, "Are you ready?"

"Yes," came the stoic reply.

"Let's do this then."

Lofty opened fire at the flashes. "Push forward," he said to Suma.

They walked steadily onward as they fired at the flashes. A shout from the poachers and the outgoing fire shifted. Lofty and Suma went to ground, still firing at the poachers.

Lofty reached for a fragmentation grenade hooked onto his webbing. They were ordered to use them as a last resort. Well, that's where they were. He pulled the pin and called, "Frag out!"

The explosion rolled across the landscape, cries of pain among it from the wounded poachers. Lofty and Suma followed it up with a sustained burst then waited.

The incoming fire tapered off and then ceased. Lofty said into his comms, "Bravo One, copy?"

"Read you, Reaper Four."

"Need a sitrep on the poachers, over. We think they're bugging out."

"Wait one, hold position."

"Roger that."

Lofty looked at Suma. "Are you all right?"

She nodded. "Yes. They will be headed to the border. We may have won this round, but the battle is far from over."

"Aye, lass, that's true."

"Reaper Four, confirm your friends are bugging out toward the north. Expect them to head across the border into Zambia."

"Roger. Knocker, you still alive?"

"That was a dumb thing to do, you stupid prick," the Brit growled.

"I take that as a yes. Are you coming across?"

"Piss off."

"Reaper Four, this is Zero, copy?"

"Roger, Zero."

"Hold position. Reapers One and Five are coming to you. Out."

"Copy, holding position. Out."

CHAPTER 2

QUI NHON, VIETNAM

"Mamba One, sitrep, over."

"Alpha One, this is Mamba One, we're in position, over."

Cara Billings tapped the tech beside her on the shoulder and said, "Get their bodycams up on the screen. Plus their tracking. I want to know where they are at all times."

"Yes, ma'am."

Normally Cara would have been with the rest of her team, but at that point in time, the former Marine and sheriff's deputy who was in her midthirties was in command of an operation in Qui Nhon, Vietnam.

Since taking up the posting with Strike Team Mamba, she'd let her short dark hair grow out a bit but remained trim with her regimented fitness routine.

Mamba's mission this time out was to intercept an illegal shipment of ivory from Africa. The shipment itself had links to terrorists in Kenya. Should the ivory be sold, the money would go into the coffers of the terrorists, and that couldn't happen.

Mamba was a team of four led by Roy Roberts, former commando. His second was Ted Clarke, once an operator in the Special Reconnaissance Regiment. The remaining two were Ollie Smith and Simon Flint, both from the Mercian Regiment.

The meet had been set on the outskirts of Qui Nhon in an abandoned suburban high-rise development. Some years previously, the developer's money had run out and construction had come to a standstill. After the passage of time, it had been returned to nature, with trees and weeds giving it the appearance of something post-apocalyptic.

"Get ISR up," Cara said calmly.

A second large screen came online, and feed came through from a UAV circling overhead. "All right, we're seeing everything now."

"Mamba is ready to execute on command."

"I've got three vehicles coming in from the east," one of the techs said.

Cara looked at a third screen. "I see them. They look to be our buyer."

The three black SUVs pulled up and ten men got out. Nine were armed, the tenth was dressed in a suit and wore sunglasses. "Can we get confirmation that Tan is on site?"

Tan was the buyer, renowned throughout the black market world for being able to acquire most things illegal.

"I have confirmation," said a voice to Cara's right.

"Mamba One, copy?"

"Mamba One reading."

"Confirmation our buyer is on site," Cara confirmed.

"Roger that, boss."

"More vehicles coming in. Three trucks this time," said the same tech who'd warned the earlier about the approaching vehicles.

"That'll be the ivory," said Cara.

"Ma'am, we have confirmation that the ship has been impounded and the crew detained at the docks."

"Good."

The trucks came to a halt and more armed men climbed out. The buyer and the seller walked toward the back of one of the trucks.

"Ma'am, we have positive identification on the seller. Thomas Abebe."

Abebe was the middleman liaising between the buyers and the terrorists. He was a shrewd businessman who kept both sides happy, but the ultimate outcome was to line his own pockets as best he could.

"Alpha One, we may have a problem," came the voice of Roberts.

"What is it, Mamba One?"

"We've picked up movement among the buildings to the north. Please advise."

"Standby," Cara replied. "Get me eyes on now."

The screen changed and after a few moments, the reason for the suspected movement became evident. "Shit," Cara growled. "Roberts, you've got visitors. Count is ten tangos. Stand down and observe."

"Roger, boss."

"Ma'am, the tangos are moving."

Suddenly the target area came alive with gunfire. As Cara watched on, men started to fall all around the vehicles. "This is a rip-off," she muttered to herself.

"They look to be professionals, boss," Roberts muttered through his comms. "What do you want us to do?"

"Remain where you are."

"Roger that."

As Cara watched, she saw Abebe and Tan go down. The shooters moved with professional efficiency. Cara turned to the person closest to her in the makeshift ops center. "See if we can get comms intercept on them. Someone this professional must have comms."

"Yes, ma'am."

Then it was over. The armed intruders picked over the corpses and shot the wounded.

"Cold," Cara said.

"Ma'am, we have intercepted some chatter."

"Play it."

"...check for more wounded and..."

"...the trucks are loaded like..."

"...them..."

"They're South African," Cara mused. "Most likely mercenaries. I want a check on all known private contractors in the area from down south."

"On it, ma'am."

It was over within minutes and the mercenaries disappeared with the trucks. "Ma'am, do you want us to follow with the UAV?"

"No, too much civilian air traffic. We'll pick them up eventually. For now, work with what we have."

"Yes, ma'am."

"Mamba One, come home."

"Roger, Mamba One out."

———

"RASSIE MARKRAM," the blonde woman said to Cara, placing the folder in front of her.

"Why do I feel that I should know that name, Paula?" Cara asked contemplatively, looking down at the file.

"He's the biggest diamond miner in Africa."

"Then why is he hiring mercenaries to kill illegal ivory traffickers and steal their ivory?" Cara wondered out loud.

"They were men from his own army."

Cara raised her eyebrows and looked up at Paula. "Own army?"

"Yes, he contracts anyone who will join him. He has three battalions."

Cara nodded. "Okay, Paula, thank you."

Cara picked up the file. On top was a picture of Markram. He was a man in his fifties, square jaw, handsome, and it appeared as though his wife was twenty years younger than him.

As Paula had said, he was the largest diamond miner in Africa and, surprise, surprise, linked to some illegal dealings in smaller countries across the continent to get what he wanted.

"What are you up to, Rassie?"

She continued poring through the intel in the folder. Markram's private army was deployed to wherever he chose to send them to carry out his nefarious agenda. His battalions were named after African animals. Lion, Rhino, and Hyena. One of his commanders, David Galloway, was a former soldier from Zimbabwe, whose father had been a soldier in the Rhodesian SAS. The others all had armed forces experience.

None of the information gave her the answers she sought regarding the motive of the ambushed buy.

Paula reappeared. Cara looked up. "What is it?"

"It might be nothing, but Markram had a meeting earlier this week with General Ignatius Omossola from Cameroon."

"The rebel leader?"

"The very same, ma'am. Omossola has been attempting to get rid of the current government for the past two years. But he's been lacking money and arms."

"Something that Markram has, and plenty of both," Cara pointed out.

Paula nodded. "We think that the money from the ivory was going to be funneled back through to the government in Cameroon. They're about broke and the millions from black market ivory would help shore up their economy."

"But why would Markram be supporting rebels in Cameroon?"

"There would have to be something in it for him," Paula said. "Something big."

Cara nodded. "We're going to have to watch him."

"Also, the French are expected to be putting peace-keepers on the ground within the next week because of the escalation of violence in the country. The UN is sending some emissaries ahead of them to pave the way."

"So, what we're guessing is that Markram foiled the sale to deprive the Cameroon government of desper-ately needed money to keep their economy afloat?"

"Yes, ma'am."

"And if they don't it will collapse, and the country will spiral into civil war?"

"That's about it."

"I need to talk to Hank Jones. We have to get eyes inside that country to see what Markram is up to. Unless I miss my guess, he's already got men in there ready to go to work."

———

CHOBE NATIONAL PARK, BOTSWANA

The Sikorsky UH-60 Black Hawk helicopter lifted off and disappeared into the distance carrying its grim cargo of dead and wounded. Two poachers dead, three wounded. According to Kayla and her two scouts, six more poachers had escaped to kill again.

Kane looked at Kayla and said, "I need someone out front who knows what they're doing."

Kayla nodded. "I will send Suma."

He looked around. "Lofty, go with Suma. Scouting."

"Roger that, boss."

Knocker stepped up beside Kane and said, "These bastards are fucking pricks, Reaper."

"Uh-huh."

"What do you think?"

"We follow them and see where they go."

"You don't want to intercept them?" Knocker was incredulous at the response.

"No, I want to know where they're going," Kane said.

"You know they aren't going to let us cross the border."

"Luis is working on it."

"Well, he needs to work faster," the Brit said.

Kane slapped him on the back. "Move out."

They followed the trail for the next few hours under the watchful gaze of the multitude of animals that resided in the park.

"Reaper One, copy?" Lofty said over the comms.

"Copy, Reaper Four."

"You'd best get up here."

"On my way." Kane looked at Knocker. "Hold the squad here."

"Roger that."

"Kayla, on me."

They walked forward through the brush to where a large acacia stood. Beneath it, leaning against the trunk was a dead man. He'd been shot in the stomach and had obviously been holding the others up. Whoever was in charge had cut their losses and shot him through the head while he rested.

Lofty held out a photo for Kane to take. "Someone wasn't as sanitized as they should have been."

Kane stared at the picture. He passed it to Kayla. "I'm not sure what I'm looking at."

It took her a matter of seconds before she said, "He's from Cameroon."

"How do you know that?" Kane asked.

"The background writing behind the woman. I'd say that was his wife."

Lofty said, "For a man to carry a picture of his wife around like that can only mean one thing."

"Military?" Kane theorized. "Or former military."

Kayla said, "Check his right wrist. A lot of Cameroon military personnel have a tattoo of a lion on their wrists."

Lofty picked up the man's hand and turned it over, locating the tattoo as suggested. "She was right."

"What the hell are Cameroon soldiers doing down

here poaching?" Kane wondered out loud. "Zero, copy?"

"Read you loud and clear, Reaper One."

"We've got Cameroon soldiers inside the wire. Have the other poachers checked when they touch down."

"Understood."

"We're Charlie Mike."

"Roger. Out."

"All right, let's keep humping."

———

MOSEKI CAMP

The fact that there were Cameroon soldiers inside the park was troubling. But not as troubling as the call Ferrero was about to get from Hank Jones at Hereford.

"Luis, balls to the wall, I hear," the big former general said. He was a bear of a man who'd served in Vietnam and now was commanding the Global Corporation. "Is Mary around anywhere?"

"I think she just stepped out, General."

"Never mind. Listen, there may be something in the wind. I just wanted to give you all a heads-up just in case you're re-tasked."

"Yes, sir."

"Cara was running a team in Vietnam. The other end of the smuggling ring you're all working. Apparently, some shit went down, and a third party came in and killed everyone."

"Did they steal the ivory, Hank?" Ferrero asked.

"Yes."

"Ivory war?"

"They were mercenaries who work for a South African diamond miner by the name of Rassie Markram."

"I've heard of him," Ferrero said.

"He was pictured meeting Ignatius Omossola in Cameroon."

Ferrero remained silent as he thought about what he'd just learned.

"Are you still there, Luis?"

"I'm here. There is something you should know. There was an incident with the poachers last night. It looks as though they are Cameroon soldiers."

"And slowly things start to fall into place," Jones grumbled. "Cameroon is about broke. The money from poaching will help put much needed funds in their accounts. They set up a sale and Markram blew it, leaving the ivory because that wasn't what he was after."

"Regime change would be my guess," Ferrero replied.

"Yes, which means Markram is after something."

"My guess too. The UN is sending a small delegation into the country. We're dispatching a security team of two with them on a fact-finding mission. The delegation is to smooth things over so that French peace-keepers can be moved in. If it doesn't work, we can expect a civil war to commence very soon."

"Who are you sending?"

"Cara."

———

NORTHERN TRANSVAAL, SOUTH AFRICA

The biggest diamond mine in the world and it was useless. Nothing was coming out of the damned cut and it was costing him over $5,000,000 a day. Rassie Markram looked at the figures once more, hoping to find something he might have missed. But he hadn't and the number was still the same.

He smashed the piece of paper up into a ball and growled. "Fucking bastard ground."

The door to the office opened and a tall, blond-headed man walked in. Markram glanced up at Galloway. "What is it?"

"Most of the advisory teams are in Cameroon already but we have a problem."

"What now?"

"The UN is sending some dignitaries into the country to try and prevent the civil war coming to hand."

"What do we know of them?" Markram asked.

"Not a lot. Just that there are two of them. They will meet with President Dawar and try to come up with a solution. Mostly it's about French peacekeepers landing the day after they arrive."

"Then we must stop them."

"How do you want to do that, sir?"

"Shoot the damn plane down."

"Are you sure that's the route you want to take?" Galloway asked.

"Just see that it's done. There are billions of dollars at stake."

"Yes, sir."

————

CHOBE NATIONAL PARK, BOTSWANA

"That's the border down there," Kayla said, as they stared at the acacia thicket. "We can't go any further."

Knocker nodded. "I guess we go home."

"Not yet," Kane said. "To operate the way they do, they must have a camp very close to the border."

"The only way to find out would be go have a look," Knocker said.

"Any volunteers?"

"I will go," said Kayla.

"Fine," said Knocker. "I will go too."

Kane nodded. "Two will do. I don't want any more. We'll monitor the border from here."

"What do you want us to do if we find the camp?" Knocker asked.

"Reach out and I'll see if we can get permission to cross over. If we can shut down their camp, then it'll go a long way to stopping the poaching on this side."

"Roger that."

They headed off the ridge and into the thicket below. Kayla walked point tracking the poachers as she went. They crossed over and broke free of the brush. The terrain grew rockier and then opened out a little with deep gullies crisscrossing the plain.

By late afternoon the sun was going down and the day was losing heat fast. Kayla said, "We should camp here for the night."

"All right. Should we risk a fire?"

"Yes, why not?"

They worked together, scraping together enough dead wood to get a fire burning. Off in the distance, Knocker heard a hyena and then another answered it. Somewhere else a lion roared and then came some other noises from the gloom. Kayla said, "The wild ones are talking among themselves tonight."

"As long as they stay away from us," Knocker replied.

"They will not bother us," Kayla replied. "We will be making too much noise of our own."

Knocker raised an eyebrow. "What? Oh. Oh right."

"Unless you don't want to fuck me and I'm getting it all wrong."

She took off her shirt and then her tank top to reveal firm, high breasts tipped with almost black nipples. She stepped forward and worked on his belt. Knocker swallowed. "Are you sure you want to do this?"

"In the anti-poaching squad, we believe that sex before battle helps us to be braver when the time comes."

Knocker cocked his head to one side. "What happens when there isn't any men around?"

She smiled at him. "We make do."

"I guess you do."

———

As they lay together by the fire, Knocker asked, "What made you get into the anti-poaching squad?"

"My husband was killed by poachers. He was a ranger. I have a daughter and I need to support her."

"So you joined for the money?"

"Yes," Kayla replied. "And because I want my daughter to grow up with the animals around her."

"How old is she?"

"Five."

"What is her name?" the Brit asked.

"Nyaga."

"That is a pretty name."

"She is a pretty girl."

A moment of silence and Kayla said, "You were a soldier, once."

"Yes."

"Not anymore?"

Knocker said, "I guess we still are. More like private contractors."

"Mercenaries?"

"A little."

She traced a finger through the hairs on his chest. "How long are you in Africa?"

"Until we finish our job."

Suddenly she stopped and put her mouth near his ear. "Someone is here."

Knocker reached for his P226. "Are you sure?"

"I think it was a mistake for us to fuck beside the fire."

"Speak for yourself," Knocker said.

"Leave your weapon. It is too late. Promise me you will do nothing."

"I promise," Knocker said reluctantly. His hand retracted and he remained still. Then men dressed in camouflage came out of the darkness and pointed their guns at them.

CHAPTER 3

ZAMBIA

They dropped Kayla's inert form beside Knocker and walked out of the small hut the pair was being held in. She'd been beaten savagely over the past couple of days and was now starting to show signs of her tough exterior cracking.

Knocker took her in his arms. He didn't know how she stood up to it. She was bleeding from the mouth and nose, and one eye was all but closed. Her pretty face was now covered in more bumps and bruises than Knocker cared to count. He'd been subjected to beatings by the Cameroon soldiers, but nothing compared to Kayla. They'd identified her as the weak link. "Hang in there, girl, they will come for us."

After being found by the poachers, they had been brought to the village where they were locked in the hut. The severe beatings on Kayla had begun on the first day, subjecting Knocker as well with sticks and gun butts. That night they had taken Kayla again.

Knocker figured they were around ten kilometers across the border. He'd heard trucks and voices, and when they took him out to beat him, he estimated there to be around twenty men in the camp.

After two days without contact, he figured Kane and the others wouldn't be too far away. All they had to do was hang on and stay alive.

———

"Sitrep, Bravo One?" Kane asked as they sheltered in a thicket of acacias on the outskirts of the poachers' camp.

"I count twenty-one targets with possibly more out of sight," Rani replied. "No sign of our friends."

"Keep scanning the camp. We'll move in five mikes whether we have them located or not."

Kane knew they were there; they'd found the place where they'd been taken. Now all they had to do was get them back.

"Reaper Five, set?"

"Roger that, Reaper. Just say the word," Brick replied.

Richard "Brick" Peters, former SEAL and security expert. Trained combat medic and the man they all looked to when they were losing blood.

Kane said, "On my word."

"Copy, standing by."

"Rani, anything?"

"Nothing as yet."

"Copy. Reaper One to all callsigns. NVGs on, clear as you go, and watch where your rounds are going. On my mark. Three...two...one...execute."

Kane came out of the brush and opened fire at the

first guard he saw. The 417 barked twice and the poacher dropped dead. Behind Kane came Lofty covering the area to his left while one of the anti-poaching squad covered right.

Lofty saw two poachers appear from behind a hut, both armed. "Contact left," he snarled and opened fire.

As soon as he heard the call, Kane swung his weapon left and shot the second poacher, the first already falling from Lofty's shots. "Clear the hut," Kane barked.

Lofty tried the door and found it open. He swept the hut and withdrew. "Clear!"

From the other side of the camp, Kane heard the other team, led by Brick, engaged with the poachers.

The fighting ebbed and flowed but the anti-poaching squad, led by Team Reaper gained the upper hand over the Cameroon soldiers. Then, with only a few huts left to clear, Lofty hit the jackpot.

He burst in and found Knocker huddled in a corner cradling Kayla in his arms. A little worse for wear, he looked up at his teammate and said, "About fucking time, Mucker."

"Reaper, I've passed Jackpot."

"Good man. What's their status?"

"Wait one."

"Status, old man?"

"I'm all right. Kayla has had a bad time of it. Get Brick over here."

"Reaper, we could use Brick."

"Copy."

Lofty gave Knocker his P226 and said, "Here, I'll be back."

Ten minutes later the camp was secure. The

poachers who weren't dead had fled into the night, leaving behind their wounded.

Brick was checking on Kayla while the rest of the anti-poaching squad secured the perimeter.

"Zero from Reaper One, over."

"Read you, Reaper One," said Ferrero.

"Camp secure. Request extract, over."

"Copy. A bird is on the way. Burn the ivory before you leave."

"Copy. Out," Kane said into his comms, "Lofty."

"Yeah, boss?"

"Grab Suma and find what you can to burn the ivory."

"Roger that."

Kane walked over to where the few wounded prisoners were being guarded by two of the anti-poaching squad. "Anyone speak English?"

No one spoke.

"If one of you can answer my questions, I will let him go."

One of them turned his head and looked at Kane.

Got you. Kane pointed at him. "Get up."

The man tried to look puzzled, but it did him no good.

Kane grabbed his shirt and dragged him to his feet in spite of the wound in his leg. The man cried out in protest, but his pleas fell on deaf ears. Kane dragged him over to a hut and sat him down outside of it. Brick came over to join them.

"What's going on, boss?"

"Our friend here is going to answer some questions."

"He looks like he wants to."

"He does, doesn't he?"

The wounded Cameroon poacher swallowed nervously.

"Why are you here?" Kane asked.

The man said nothing.

"I know you speak English," Kane informed him. "Answer my questions or I'll turn you over to the women. After what you lot did to their boss, I doubt you'll see morning."

"Why do you think we are here?" the man spat.

Kane nodded. "The fact that you speak English tells me that you are an officer. You command here?"

He ignored the question.

"Why are Cameroon soldiers poaching ivory?"

"Because we need the money."

"Did your government order this?"

Nothing.

"Listen, what you do now has ramifications on the outcome. I can get you put in prison here—which is fucked for you—or I can get you put in a Belgian one which, I believe, would be far more preferable. Your choice."

"My country is almost broke. They need the money. The banks are starting to shut so people cannot get their money from them. Cameroon is only one step away from civil war. If we cannot get money it is doomed."

Kane nodded. "Brick."

They walked away a few steps. "Send that information to Luis. I'm guessing he'll pass it on to whoever."

"Roger that," the former SEAL replied. "What now?"

"We go home and get some rest."

———

MOSEKI CAMP

Mary Thurston was mulling over the information she'd just received. The team commander was in her early forties and long, dark hair was tied back. She wore jungle BDUs and sipped on a beer as she reread the paperwork. "This can't be fucking true."

She picked up the satellite phone from her desk and dialed.

"Mary? Are you wrapping things up?"

"This op, General," she replied.

"What can I do for you?"

"For starters you can tell me what this bullshit memo is that I just read," she growled.

"I was wondering when you'd get around to that," he said. There was a hint of craftiness in his voice.

"Why didn't you fucking tell me?"

"I did. You just read it."

"This is bullshit."

"I'm dying, Mary. Someone has to take over Global. You're it."

"That's crap; you're as tough as anyone I know."

"Not this time. The doctors tell me I have early-stage Alzheimer's. It's time to pass the baton. You're it. I want you on a plane home within the week."

"Hank—"

"Don't keep saying this is bullshit, Mary. You're stronger than that. It's my time. I've had a good run."

"Yes, sir."

"You will need to pick a successor," Jones said.

"Luis could step up—"

"No, he stays where he is. Besides, I doubt he would want it anyway. Choose another."

Thurston thought for a moment. "There is another I would trust to do it."

"Fine, send me the recommendation and I'll approve it with the board. Just as long as it isn't that fucking Limey."

Thurston smiled at the mention of Knocker. Then her face changed again.

"I'm sorry, Hank," Thurston said.

"It is what it is. Take care, Mary."

"You too, sir."

The call disconnected and she reached for her cell. Another number and a voice said, "What's up, Mary?"

"My office, Luis, now."

"Yes, ma'am."

He was there within two minutes.

"It sounds urgent."

"Hank Jones is stepping down within the week. Alzheimer's."

"Shit."

"He's moving me up to take overall charge of Global," Thurston said. "We discussed—"

"Wait, before you say it, I don't want it. Operations is what I do. I'm happy there, it's where I'm best suited."

"I'm glad you feel that way, Luis, because that's what Hank and I decided. Which still leaves someone to take overall command."

"I'm guessing you have someone in mind?"

"I do. Now, tell me about our latest operation."

———

OVER SUD, CAMEROON

Cara closed her eyes and waited for the missile to hit the Cessna Citation as it passed over the Sud. Beside her sat Roy Roberts, the leader of Strike Team Mamba. She'd already called out a warning to the others upon noticing it coming up from the jungle below.

Impact was imminent and she wished she had a chance to say goodbye to Jimmy before she died. Her fingers dug deep into the armrests, her hands cramping almost immediately. Beside her, she heard Roberts say, "Well, this is fucked."

Then nothing. Blackness and quiet.

SUD, CAMEROON

Colonel Moumi Onana watched the Cessna fall from the sky. Actually, it was more of a controlled crash, and he had to assume that the pilots were well trained as it disappeared into the jungle some twenty kilometers away from where the rebel colonel stood. Onana reached for the radio and said, "The plane has gone down in the jungle to the north of my position. I want all teams to converge on that point immediately. Kill any survivors. Onana, out."

The colonel walked back toward his Jeep and climbed in beside his driver. He nodded stiffly in the direction of the plane and the Jeep lurched forward. It would take them at least an hour to reach the crash site.

CARA GROANED and undid her seat belt. Beside her, Roberts did the same. He said, "Are we dead or alive?"

"I think we're alive," Cara replied.

"If that's the case then we need to assess the situation and get the fuck out of here, boss."

"Roger that."

Apart from a few cuts and bruises, the two operators were relatively unscathed. They checked on the UN detail and found both men alive. The pair were French. Sacha Corbin had a dislocated shoulder which Roberts immediately relocated, and Emile Allard's left arm was broken. Both had cuts and bruises as well.

The pilots on the other hand, having done their utmost to put the plane down safely, were dead thanks to a tree branch that had come through the cockpit.

Cara tried the radio while Roberts triaged the two UN officers. "Mayday...mayday...mayday..."

It was no good, however, the radio was dead. She walked over to Roberts. "The radio is fucked. How are our friends?"

"We are fine," Allard assured her. "What the hell happened?"

"We were shot down by a missile."

His eyebrows shot up. "A missile?"

"That's right. Someone didn't want you to reach your destination."

"Oh, my Lord."

Cara nodded. "Roy, find our packs."

"Yes, boss."

He hurried over to the luggage compartment part of the plane. Cara looked around at the thick jungle, still bewildered at how they'd actually survived. Roberts returned moments later with their bags.

Cara opened hers and started taking out equipment

she would need. The two Frenchmen watched in bewilderment as the pair stripped down to their underwear and pulled on their Synoprathetic suits.

"What are they?" Corbin asked.

"They are called Synoprathetic bodysuits," Cara replied. "They are bulletproof up to a certain point. They help keep us alive if we get shot."

"You're expecting to get shot?" Allard asked, more than a little concerned.

Cara pulled her pants back on and said, "I'm not planning on it, but this way we're prepared."

She put on her shirt and shoes and then her body armor. Corbin said, "You both make me feel quite secure—oh fuck me."

Cara had taken out her suppressed LWRC M6A2 assault carbine. "Don't worry, it's just a precaution against lions and shit like that."

Behind her Roberts was preparing himself in the same way.

By the time they were finished, they discarded their duffels and put on backpacks. Then Cara took out a satellite phone and tried to turn it on.

Nothing.

"Yeah, we've got a big fucked up problem."

———

MOSEKI CAMP

"The plane went down there," Ferrero said, stabbing his finger at the map. "In the Sud. From intel that's been gathered there were four of them still alive and they were mobile."

"Where are they headed?" Kane asked.

"We think, Ebolowa," Ferrero replied. "Right in the middle of rebel territory."

Rani said, "Right at this time, they have at least five teams of rebels closing in on them. If they can get through the net, they might have a chance of making it."

"When do we go?" Knocker asked.

"Not you," Rosanna Morales, the team doctor protested. "You're on bed rest."

"Do I look like I'm in bloody bed?"

"You are incorrigible."

"Yes, ma'am. What you said."

"Is there a way of getting us inside that net?" Kane asked.

"No," Rani said. "You could get close, maybe open a doorway for them to slip through. But the only way of getting you out after that is from Ebolowa."

"Shit."

"Be aware, news of this is all over the Cameroon media networks. Rebel forces are building outside the capital, ready for an assault. French peacekeepers will be on the ground soon, but it may not be soon enough."

"If you ask me, it may just be six a one, half a dozen the other," Knocker said.

They all remained quiet.

Knocker shook his head. "I fucking miss that big prick. Both the leaders are about the same. One encourages poaching and the other kills thousands to get where he wants to go. They both deserve each other."

Ferrero said, "Neither the government of Great Britain nor the European Union supports the hostile takeovers of sovereign nations."

"Fuck me. Let's get our people back."

"Get ready. You'll be dropped in tonight."

"That's more like it," Knocker said, his voice dripping with sarcasm. "A night drop into the jungle. What could possibly go wrong?"

————

SUD, CAMEROON

Onana looked at the wreckage of the plane and spat on the damp earth in disgust. Only the pilots were there, the others having cheated death and escaped. He turned to his second in command and said, "Look for any sign."

"Yes, sir."

Onana's radio operator approached him. "Sir, you must hear this."

He turned the volume up on the radio and the colonel listened. Rebel forces were surrounding the capital and preparing to attack it. Meanwhile, French forces were building along the border, and their recon units along with a unit of Foreign Legion troops, were ready to deploy ahead of the main force.

Onana knew that the capital must be taken before the French peacekeepers moved into his country. For if they did, and the rebels attacked the French troops, then civil war would become war with a foreign power.

"Sir, we have found tracks," a soldier called over to Onana. "There are four of them. They're headed northeast."

The colonel nodded. "Gather the men."

"Yes, sir."

Onana turned to his radio operator. "Radio the other groups. Give them our coordinates and the direction the survivors are taking."

"Yes, sir."

"And tell them if they get away, I will cut out their hearts myself."

"Yes, sir."

———

"DANGER CLOSE. MOVEMENT AHEAD," Roberts whispered as he reappeared through the undergrowth ahead of Cara.

She turned and whispered urgently. "Get off the trail. Now."

The small group slipped into the undergrowth, the thick foliage springing back into place when they disappeared. Moving slowly, they had been walking for two hours. To rush was to die.

At first, Cara heard nothing except for the buzzing of insects all around her. Then came the voices. Distant at first and then growing steadily closer.

The first man appeared on the trail, armed with an AK-74. Then came the rest, all in line. There were ten of them. Joking, happy, careless.

Cara watched them carefully as the men slipped past them on the trail. She gripped her M6 tightly, ready to fire. Then as the last one walked by, a straggler, unknowing that they were there, she started to feel relieved.

Until Allard sneezed.

The rear security man stopped and turned toward the jungle where Allard was hiding. Cara clenched her jaw in anger, gripping her weapon.

The rebel's head weaved left and right as he tried to see through the undergrowth. Then he stopped, eyes widened, and his mouth opened to shout a warning.

Then Cara shot him through the side of his head with her M6. Blood and brain sprayed the foliage and the rebel dropped to the ground in the middle of the track. Roberts materialized from the jungle nearby and moved quickly to drag the dead man into the green maw.

Then they waited in silence before loud voices could be heard getting closer. They were returning in search of their friend.

Then they appeared.

"Do it," Cara said in a low voice.

Both opened fire with their suppressed M6s. The rebels were cut down by the deliberate fire. First two, then four, then six.

Then the remaining rebels opened fire, their bullets cutting through the jungle foliage like a giant with a machete.

Cara shifted her aim and shot another rebel down low. He cried out in pain and fell back.

Further along, Roberts did the same and before long, the remaining rebels were down. But there was no time to dally. Anyone close enough would have heard the commotion. Cara stepped out onto the trail and said, "Roy, checkpoint."

"Boss."

He disappeared along the trail, and Cara gathered the other two together. Her face said it all. "The next time you feel like sneezing, cut your fucking nose off or you'll get us fucking killed. Christ, fuck me."

"I couldn't—"

"You'd better fucking help it if you want to get out of here," she said savagely, cutting him off. "Now, follow the track, and do it fast."

———

Onana looked at the dead men on the trail and hissed in frustration. The sun was starting to go down over the jungle to the west and there had been no inroads made in the search for the ones they were chasing. A soldier came up behind him. "Sir?"

He turned around. "Yes?"

"The whole patrol is dead. No one survived."

"It is better for them that they are," he said bitterly. "Are they still headed in the same direction?"

"Yes, sir."

"Get our best men out front. I want them run to ground like the cheetah hunting the gazelle. Do it, now."

"Yes, sir."

———

NORTHERN TRANSVAAL, SOUTH AFRICA

Galloway entered Markram's office, ready to convey both good and bad news. He got the good out of the way first because there was no other way. "The plane was shot down by Omossola's rebels."

"I can tell there is more, David."

"There were survivors. Colonel Onana is currently pursuing them through the Sud."

Markram nodded. "I think I need to take control of a few things. Especially now that the French are that much closer to putting troops on the ground to shore up the government. Have Rhino Battalion ready to deploy. You will lead them."

"What is our target?"

"The airport. You will secure it. Omossola will support you."

"Yes, sir."

"Good luck, David."

"Thank you, sir."

CHAPTER 4

"All call signs check in," Kane said in a soft voice.

"Reaper Three, checking in."

"Reaper Four, checking in."

"Reaper Five, checking in."

"Copy. Zero, this is Reaper One. All callsigns are down and rallying my position."

"Copy, Reaper One. Read your last loud and clear."

"Roger, out."

At least the team was down in one piece, that was something. All were wearing the new Synoprathetic suits under their combat fatigues as well as body armor and SAS jungle hats. They were heavily armed. Kane and Brick had jumped with the M6A2. Knocker with the designated marksman's Heckler and Koch 417, while Lofty had gone in heavy with an M249 SAW.

All carried small arms and grenades, both fragmentation and smoke, along with claymores. Put together with eyes in the sky. No air cover, just satellite.

Once they were all grouped, Kane reached out to Rani. "Bravo One, copy?"

"Read you loud and clear, Reaper One."

"I need a bearing, over."

"Reaper One, target is four klicks to your northeast, over."

"Copy. Reaper One out." Kane turned to the others. "Knocker, on point. Brick, rear security. We'll swap after an hour. Move out."

They made slow progress through the darkness and by morning were still two klicks behind their target. But that wasn't their only problem. A group of unidentified tangos were closing in on the rear of the four crash survivors. And there was no way to warn them.

On the good news front, it was almost certain, judging by the way they were moving, that Cara and Strike Team Mamba leader, Roy Roberts were still alive. Kane felt relief.

As the sun rose, the jungle came alive. Animals, insects, birds.

And men.

Brick was on point when he came across them. Their satellite cover was gone, and they'd been moving parallel to the rebel column without knowing it and almost ran into them. Kane was in the vanguard when the voice came over the comms. "Danger close. Hold."

They all went to ground and waited while Brick watched them from up close. Fifty rebel soldiers made their way along the trail past the former SEAL who was hidden in the undergrowth.

Fifteen minutes later, it was all clear.

Kane came forward and settled in beside Brick. The former SEAL said, "We've now got about fifty rebels between us and them. What do you want to do?"

"Trail them for the moment. We're still a good twelve hours from Ebolowa. If Cara is with them, she'll have a rear security out and they'll pick up their approach before going to ground. If not, we just hope they can hang on. Let's move."

―――――

"WE'VE GOT rebels coming up on our six," Roberts told Cara four hours later.

"How many?" she asked.

"Too many, boss."

Cara looked around at the jungle. "All right, time to go quiet."

She walked over to Allard and Corbin. "How are you two traveling?"

Corbin nodded. "I'm all right."

"Arm is playing up a bit," Allard told her.

Truth be known, Cara had a feeling it was more than just a bit. She reached into her pack and pulled out a small bundle. She took out a small syrette of morphine. "Here."

She stabbed him with it, and he looked at her. "What—"

"Morphine. I was saving it. Right now, though, we need to take cover. And no fucking sneezing."

They slipped into the jungle and waited in silence. Ten minutes later the first of the rebel soldiers started past. Cara had moved them all well off the trail before moving herself and Roberts closer to keep an eye on the soldiers as they passed.

Once they were gone, Cara said, "We need to change our direction."

Roberts grinned. "Got a map?"

"Got a beer?"

They were just about to move when Cara sensed rather than saw movement from the trail once more. Using hand signals the two operators settled down and watched as a single figure appeared, cautiously moving along the trail in front of them. The figure stopped and looked around. Then she heard a distinctly British voice say, "Reaper One, hold position. Reaper Two, are you bloody coming out any time soon?"

Cara rose to her feet and walked out of the under-growth. "I think I'm in love with you, Knocker."

"That'll have to wait," he said with a grin, his teeth showing white through the greens of his face paint. "Reaper One, I have Reaper Two with me. Holding position."

"Roger. On my way."

Knocker gave Cara a hug and said, "Lives of a cat, woman."

"Only just." She turned to the jungle and waved Roberts forward. "I think I used them all up."

"Who made it with you?"

"Roberts and the two French emissaries. The poor pilots got killed getting us down. Surface to air missile."

"Someone really didn't want you to get there."

"That's it."

The others emerged from the jungle while Kane, Lofty, and Brick came up the trail. Like Knocker, Kane gave Cara a hug. "Are you all right?"

"I'll live."

"Brick, check our French friends. Knocker, set up a forward OP. Lofty, rear security."

"Roger, boss."

For the next few minutes, Cara filled Kane in on

what had happened. In return, he told her of the theories circulating about what was going on with the rebels.

Once he was finished, Kane said, "We need to push on to Ebolowa. It's the only place they can extract us."

"Middle of rebel territory."

"And still eight hours away."

"Shit. Do you have a map?" Cara asked.

Kane dug into his pack and found what he needed. Cara took it and started to look it over. She stabbed her finger on the map and said, "Here. Small village. They can extract us from there. Southwest and only a short jump over the border."

Kane stared at her. "That's about ten hours back the other way."

"More like twelve." Cara looked at her watch. "We need to get moving."

"Reaper One to Zero."

"Zero copies."

"We've picked up our lost sheep, over."

"Good to hear, Reaper One."

"Be advised there's been a change of plan." He gave them the news and coordinates for the new extraction point.

"Roger that. Your call. Out."

Kane turned to Cara. "Let's get you both on comms. By the way, it's good to have you back."

"The jury is still out on that one," she replied dryly.

———

"WE HAVE LOST THEM, SIR," the young rebel lieutenant regretfully informed Onana. "The forward scouts say they have lost their trail."

The colonel nodded. "It was always a possibility

since he'd been pushing his men faster. Still, it didn't make him any happier." He said, "They are behind us somewhere. Radio Djoum. Tell him to get one of his helicopters up and sweep the jungle to the south of us. Get everyone turned around. We must find them."

"Yes, sir."

Onana stared at the jungle and grabbed his weapon tighter as anger coursed through him. Then he took a deep breath and let it out slowly. "We will find them."

———

DOUALA INTERNATIONAL AIRPORT, CAMEROON

Cesar Hassane parked the baggage cart in the large hangar and climbed out. The sun was going down and an orange hue hung over Douala to the west, the capital of Cameroon's Littoral Region.

He looked at his watch and nodded. Two more minutes and his shift would finish. He walked to the hangar opening and looked out across the runways and beyond. To his left were two armed guards who, since the increased rebel activity, were part of the beefed-up security ordered by President Dawar.

Suddenly they looked concerned, and one reached for his radio. Cesar could hear their raised voices and then watched on as they unslung their weapons.

The baggage handler was now becoming nervous.

His heart beat faster and he looked around, trying to work out what was happening. Then he heard airplane engines. Not the high-powered ones of a jet, rather the dull thrum of propellers. He looked skyward and saw the C-130s lining up to land. Not one, not two, but three, all line astern. They were coming in steep and fast, clearly handled by experienced pilots who'd flown into war zones before. Except what they were doing was decidedly more dangerous, for if the first or second stuffed the landing then the others would crash into it.

But the first one touched down with success, so did the second, the third right behind it. The planes didn't taxi, they stopped as fast as they could, their rear ramps already lowering.

Then, as Hassane watched on, the aircraft began to disgorge their passengers.

Ninety to a plane, two hundred and seventy all up. They were what was classed at the forward element of Rhino Battalion. The rest would follow when the airport was secure. All up, there would be around 800 men on the ground.

Gunfire erupted and Hassane watched as the two airport guards fell before they could recover from the surprise of what they were witnessing.

Panic filled the baggage handler as he ducked back in behind the wall near the door opening. More gunfire rattled out followed by some explosions. Hassane could hear commanders barking orders.

For a moment he thought they might have been the French peacekeepers rumored to be coming. But the deaths of the guards answered that. But if they weren't French, then who the hell were they?

———

GALLOWAY BARKED orders to his commanders as they came down the ramp of the lead C-130. Every man had his own mission to complete as they moved to secure the airport. Hangars must be cleared, the terminal as well, and the control tower to secure. That was the job of his section.

"Brendan, on me," Galloway snapped.

He was joined by his radio operator who fell into step beside him. Already gunfire could be heard across the apron. Galloway saw two guards fall and then an explosion near a fuel tanker killed more.

"Brendan, remind the commanders we don't want the fucking airport destroyed."

"Yes, sir," replied Brendan Evans as he proceeded to radio instructions to the other squads.

Ahead of the two men ran two squads of five men each. They were commanded by former sergeants of the South African armed forces. Their target was a tall building, shaped like a martini glass, at the edge of the apron.

Two guards appeared at the door leading to an internal elevator and stairwell.

They were armed.

They died.

The two lead Rhino operators fired their FN SCAR rifles and the two men dropped.

Then the assault upward began.

Galloway looked at his watch. If everything was going to plan, the outskirts of the city should be being attacked by rebels, as was the capital of Cameroon itself.

"Sir, message for you."

Galloway took the handset from the radio operator. "What is it?"

"Sir, the terminal has a lot of civilians inside it."

"Do what you can. Just try not to kill too many. Especially foreigners. The last thing we need is for you to kill Europeans or Americans."

"Yes, sir."

Galloway entered the base of the control tower and started for the stairwell. He stepped over two more guards and heard firing from near the top.

One he'd reached the control room it was already secured. He looked around the room at the frightened faces. "Who is in charge?"

"I am," said a man who stepped forward tentatively.

"Good. A prompt answer. Now, let's hope you act as quickly. The runways are closed. Divert all air traffic to other airports. No one lands here unless I say so."

"Sir, we have one plane, Delta Four-Oh-Five which is almost out of fuel. To divert it would be disastrous."

Galloway stared at him for several moments contemplating his answer. Finally, he said, "Land it. Divert the rest."

"Thank you, sir."

The Rhino commander turned to his radio operator. "Inform all commanders of the inbound plane. Then put me in contact with the other planes."

"Yes, sir."

Galloway looked out the window and turned to get the full 360-degree view that the tower offered. Already he could see dead security personnel and smoke rising from various hangars. Then the calls started coming in. "Resistance is minimal."

———

MOSEKI CAMP

"Shit has just hit the fan big time in Cameroon," Mary Thurston said to Ferrero. "There are reports of a large rebel push on the capital and the international airport."

"Sign of desperation," Ferrero said. "Not waiting for the French to put troops on the ground."

"It doesn't look like they'll be doing it, either," Thurston informed him. "They're going to use some Foreign Legion troops, elements of the Second Foreign Parachute Regiment to evacuate some foreign nationals. They've asked for our assistance should it be required."

"What did you say?"

"I told them our team was downrange at the moment and we would help if at all possible. Speaking of which, how are we looking?"

"The team is making good time considering." He pointed to the large screen. "It's almost dark and they're still about six hours from their target for extract."

"What are the two groups of dots behind them?"

"Rebels. The first group numbers about thirty forward scouts. We figure they're like the rebel pursuit team. The ones with the most endurance. They're eating into the gap like it was a Sunday lunch. The others are barely keeping up, but there're around two hundred in that group. We're about to lose satellite, and the first group is almost on top of them."

"Sweet Mother of God. Can we get anything into them?"

"Not until they reach the village."

"I take it that you have a helicopter on standby?"

"I have a Chinook and an MH-6 gunship to provide them with cover should they need it."

"Let's hope they don't."

There was movement behind them, and Kayla appeared. They turned to look at her. She still moved stiffly but was looking better each day and the swelling was going down. "Are they all right?" she asked.

"They are in a tight situation but it's nothing they haven't been in before," Thurston said.

"Can my people and I help?" she asked.

They stared at her and realized she was serious. Ferrero shook his head. "Thank you, but no. This is a little different than tracking poachers."

"It is all killing," Kayla said. "My women are quite good at it."

"That might be so, but you are needed here in Botswana," Thurston said. "Have a team put together for an operation tonight. It will be in the field for a couple of days patrolling toward the Zimbabwe Hwange park."

"Might I ask what the point of the patrol is?"

"There has been a herd of elephants sighted close to the border. If they venture across then it will draw poachers in for miles. Pack extra ammo and send three squads instead of one."

"Yes, ma'am."

"There is one other thing. I am to be replaced as commander. You will be informed when the new commander arrives. I'm quite certain you'll be able to work with them without any problem."

"I'm sorry to hear that but I look forward to working with your replacement."

Suddenly the comms speaker lit up with Knocker's voice.

"Contact! Contact! Contact!"

———

KNOCKER WAS TRYING to pick targets as best he could in the gloom as the rebel force came up behind him. "What the fuck was that, Bravo One?" he demanded as he dropped out a magazine and replaced it.

"We just lost our satellite feed, Reaper Three," Rani explained.

"Lofty, get the fuck back here with that SAW. I've got natives coming out of my fucking ass back here."

"On my way, Knocker."

Knocker reached for a fragmentation grenade and pulled the pin. He threw it around twenty meters and forgot about it as he started firing again.

The grenade detonated in the undergrowth eliciting shrieks of pain from unseen rebels. Down on one knee, Knocker felt a bullet pluck at the sleeve of his clothing, while around him branches and leaves rained to the jungle floor, cut through by the incoming rounds.

"Here we fucking go again," Knocker growled, images flashing through his mind of a hill in Sierra Leone.[1] "Ladies and gents, this is getting fucking hairy back here."

"On my way, Buddy," Brick said in his comms.

Suddenly Lofty was beside him and the SAW started to chatter with business like intent. If the jungle was getting cut to pieces before, the effect of the SAW was that of a lawn mower as it sent everything folding over.

Knocker threw another grenade. "Frag out!"

It exploded with good effect as the Brit commenced firing once more.

Then Brick appeared. Knocker said, "Throw smoke."

The former SEAL did as he was told and the gloom of the almost dark became murkier still.

"Sitrep, Reaper Three," Kane said over the comms.

"Get out of here, we'll catch you up. Keep moving."

"No, we need to set up a base of fire," Lofty snarled.

"I'm on my way," Kane said.

Moments later, both he and Roberts appeared, and had Cara left to escort the French dignitaries out of harm's way.

"Right," Kane said, "start folding back from the left."

And so it began. First, Brick. He withdrew and organized a new base of fire. As he set up, Lofty folded back to take up a position alongside him. Just like dominoes the rest followed, and once the maneuver was complete, they repeated it again.

"Throw grenades!" Kane shouted, and every man on the line threw fragmentation grenades out.

The explosions rocked the jungle as the team fell back again, this time they kept running, trying to put distance between themselves and their pursuers.

"Knocker, claymores."

"You don't fucking want much," the Brit fired back at his commander.

"I'll cover you," Lofty said.

"Too easy," Kane said. "Catch up when you're done."

So, with Lofty providing cover, Knocker put out three claymores then they settled down in the jungle and waited the few minutes for the rebels to regroup and come after them.

And it *was* only minutes before they appeared, hurrying with disregard for their safety. Then Knocker detonated the claymores.

They both ran.

———

THE ONE HOUR they were from their extract felt like ten. Pushing hard through the jungle, with the rebels close behind, every now and then the team would set a delaying claymore to slow their pursuers' progress.

Kane said over the comms, "Ammo check."

"I'm about fucked on ammo," Knocker said matter of fact.

"All right. Cara, how are you for ammo?"

"Three mags, Reaper."

"Lofty?"

"About screwed."

"Brick?"

"Two mags and whatever is left in the weapon."

"I've got three plus," Roberts replied.

"All right, you and Cara pull rear security. Everyone give them whatever spare grenades you have. Claymores?"

"Yeah, no," Knocker said.

"All right. I'll take point. Brick, Knocker, NVGs to Cara and Roy. Then look after our French friends. Move out."

The going wasn't as fast as it should have been, but the rebels had slowed as well, the claymores making them wary of more. The team pushed through the jungle until they reached the village and their extract point.

"Reaper One to Zero, over."

"Copy, Reaper One."

"We're at our extract, over."

"Copy. Birds are on the way."

The village was small and consisted of numerous grass and mud huts. Everything was quiet and it didn't take long to realize that the village was deserted. "They must have heard we were coming," Knocker said. "Hell seems to follow everywhere we go."

"Set up a defensive position," Kane said. "Just in case the helicopters don't get here in time."

They hunkered down, divvied up the remaining ammunition, and waited. For whichever arrived first: the wave of rebels or the helicopters. Cara looked at her watch. It would be daylight soon. The journey had taken longer than expected, especially with the running fight.

"You all right?" Kane asked her.

"Yes."

"Big thing, going down in a plane."

"Damn scary," she replied. "I thought I was dead."

"Breed you Marines tough," he replied with a rakish grin.

"Apparently so."

"Heads up, we got movement." It was Roberts's voice over the comms.

Suddenly there were exploding freight trains being thrown at them as mortar rounds started to impact the village. Everyone's comms lit up with reports of incoming fire. Kane said in a calm voice, "Fall back to the center of the village. Do it now."

The center of the village was open around a couple of water troughs where the previous residents had watered their animals. The team used them for cover and put the French dignitaries into the solid-looking mud structure.

Kane said to Roberts, "Take care of the French. Don't let anyone into that building. Everyone, single shots only. Make what you have count. Strobes on."

Dirt rained down upon them as more mortar rounds

landed nearby. Then just as suddenly as it had started, the noise ceased. Next would come the rebels.

"Contact!" It was Cara who opened fire first when she saw two rebels filing between some grass huts. Then Brick as he saw the same thing on the east side. Before they knew it, they were engaged with a far superior force with better fighters than they were given credit for.

They pushed forward into the kill zone and acted like sponges, soaking up bullets that the team couldn't spare.

"Grenade!" Knocker shouted.

They dropped down and took cover.

The fragmentation grenade exploded and showered them with dirt once more. Kane said into his comms. "Zero, how far out is that helicopter?"

"Should be there short—"

BRRRRPPPP! The sound of twin miniguns ripping the early morning apart was the best sound Kane had heard in a while. The helicopter roared overhead seemed to turn on its nose and came back for another gun run.

Kane said, "Zero, forget my last. The cavalry just arrived."

After two more runs, the rebels pulled back and the Chinook came in for the pickup. Five minutes later they were all on board and the helicopters retreated into the dawn.

---

1. See Cold Hand of Death

CHAPTER 5

MOSEKI CAMP, TWO DAYS LATER

"You wanted to see me, ma'am?" Cara asked entering Thurston's temporary office.

Thurston nodded. "Yes, take a seat."

With that Cara knew it was serious so sat down and waited for her commander to continue.

"How are you feeling?"

Cara shrugged. "I'm okay. Rosanna gave me a clean bill of health."

"Ready to get back to work? Rested?"

"Yes, ma'am."

"Good. I have news for you but—"

There was a knock at the door, and it opened with a squeak. Ferrero walked in followed by Kane. Thurston nodded. "Good, now we can begin."

Ferrero went around the desk and stood by Thurston while Kane leaned against the wall and waited.

Thurston said, "While we were backs to the wall, I

had a call from Hank Jones. He's been diagnosed with Alzheimer's and is stepping away from Global."

"Oh, no." Cara was aghast, a hand moving to cover her mouth which hung open.

Kane's expression was grim, but he remained silent.

Thurston continued. "This is going to lead to some changes. I'm leaving tomorrow to take up his position back in Hereford."

Cara frowned and looked at Ferrero. "You getting your old job back, Luis?"

He shook his head. "I told Mary she could go as long as she didn't expect me to take over. She agreed."

"Then who?"

"You," said Kane before anyone else could. "It's the only thing that makes sense."

"No," she said, shaking her head. "Not me, I couldn't do it."

"You'd better learn," Thurston said. "There's no one else I want for the position. Reaper, I hope you don't have a problem?"

"Not me."

"Do I get a say?" Cara asked.

"Only by saying yes. Listen, you've been in the field, you know everyone, plus you can command. Your decision making is top class."

Cara suddenly felt overwhelmed. "I don't know what to say." She was glad to be sitting down.

"Just say yes, so I can leave everyone in good hands. Then I can update you on everything before I leave. And if you have problems, Luis is here, and I'm only a phone call away. However, I think you'll hit the ground running."

Cara nodded. "Fine. Yes."

"Good, now, let's get started."

———

"You're having a laugh, aren't you?" Knocker said.

Kane shook his head. "No."

"Fuck a duck. Oh, well, at least they got someone decent for the job. How do you feel about taking orders from her?"

"I don't have a problem with that."

"Hey, what's the news out of Cameroon?"

"The rebels are in control of a good chunk of the country. The president has skipped, and they've started cleansing his supporters and those they think are supporters. It's a damn slaughter." Kane shook his head. "The Foreign Legion guys have been working around the clock pulling out foreign nationals even though they've been coming under fire. They lost a team yesterday in the Sud, not far from where we were."

"Poor bastards."

Kane nodded. "Gather the others, we're going to have a few beers to see the boss off."

"Sounds good to me." Knocker thought for a moment and said, "Who are we going to replace Cara with? I'd hate to be operating an even number."

Kane said, "While we're here, I was thinking once Kayla is back on her feet, then maybe her."

Knocker stared at him.

"What?"

"She's already back on her feet, but I'm not sure she is up to what we do after what happened to her."

Kane nodded. "I'll get the doc to talk to her and we'll see what she comes up with. If she says no, then we'll come up with another plan."

"They treated her badly, Reaper. She went through hell."

"I know."

Knocker said. "And there wasn't a fucking thing I could do about it. But you know what? She's the fucking toughest woman I've ever seen."

Kane patted Knocker on the back. "Yeah."

They heard a soft footfall behind them in the doorway and turned to see Kayla standing there. She was wearing camo pants and a white tank top. About her waist was a belt with a lion's head buckle, and on her thigh was strapped a holster containing a handgun. Knocker looked at her. "Kayla, I—"

He stopped.

Kane said, "I'll see you in the rec room for that beer after."

"Yeah, I'll be right behind you."

"Take your time."

Once Kane was gone, Kayla walked over to the Brit and stood in front of him. He said, "I'm sorry, Kayla."

She took his hand. "It is not your fault, Raymond."

"I can't help feeling that way."

Kayla squeezed his hand. "I am fine...or I will be."

"Do you feel like a beer?"

"Of course, beer fixes everything."

"I wish it did."

———

BOTSWANA/ZIMBABWE BORDER

Suma looked down at the elephant and said, "It's been dead for two days."

Ollie Smith looked at Simon Flint and shook his head. "I don't know why fuckers want to do this to such magnificent creatures."

"Money, my friend."

"Is it the same bastards who were in the Chobe?" Smith asked Suma.

She crouched beside the elephant and shook her head. "No." Suma was twenty-one and already an experienced anti-poaching squad member. She'd been at it for four years and knew exactly what she was doing. "These come from across the border."

"Just what the boss was afraid of," Smith said. "Coming out of the park. Call it in, Simon."

Hearing hurried treads, they turned as one of the other squad members jogged up. She started rapidly talking to Suma, forgetting to use English. Once she was done, Suma said, "Radio the other squads, have them come here."

"What's going on?" Flint asked.

Suma turned to Ollie Smith. "There is a problem. Come."

They followed Suma, the rest of the squad trailed along behind. They walked about 500 meters before Smith saw it. A Land Rover, windows shot out, and bullet holes all through it. Beside it lay the bodies of two men, both Black, natives.

Suma said, "There were three others. The poachers took them."

Flint looked through the vehicle and in the back, he found the camera gear. He looked for his friend. "Some kind of camera crew."

Smith pressed the transmit button on his comms. "Rani, you there, luv?"

"If it is the elusive Bravo One you are looking for, Mamba Three, then, yes, I'm here."

"Point taken, boss. We've come across an issue out here."

"Send traffic."

"It looks like a camera crew stumbled across our poachers." He went on to relay what they'd found.

Rani said, "Standby, Mamba Three."

———

MOSEKI CAMP

Rani found Thurston and Cara talking together. Both women were on their second beers as they discussed the anti-poaching squad.

"Ma'am, can I have a word?" Rani asked Thurston.

The former general shook her head. "I'm off the clock. Talk to your new boss."

She turned to Cara. "Ma'am, it looks like the anti-poaching team has come across an issue."

She relayed to Cara what she had been told. The new team commander nodded. "Let's go."

On her way out with Thurston, she signaled Ferrero, and he joined her. "Problem, Cara?"

"Could be."

When they reached their ops center, she put on a headset and said, "Rani, see if you can find out who is in that area?"

"Yes, ma'am."

"Reaper—" She stopped herself. "Bravo calling Mamba Three, over."

"Mamba Three, here, ma'am."

"What have you got?"

"Boss, we stumbled across an elephant that had been slaughtered by poachers. While we were looking, one of the squad found a shot up Land Rover. Two dead and they're telling us three missing."

"Copy. Wait one."

Cara looked at Thurston and Ferrero. "That doesn't sound like straight up poachers. If it was, they would have just shot the crew and left them."

Thurston nodded. "I agree. What do you propose to do? It's your call."

Cara said, "Mamba Three, who is your number one on the anti-poaching team?"

"Suma, boss."

"Put her on."

"This is Suma?"

"Suma, I want you to lead a squad after the poachers. Do not engage. The others will follow you once the rest of Mamba is on the ground. Understood?"

"Yes, boss."

"This is just recon. I want to know where they have crossed the border."

"Yes, boss."

"Mamba Three, copy?"

"I'm here, boss."

"Did you get that?"

"Roger that."

"I'll have Roy and Ted airborne as soon as. Hold position until they arrive. Relay your coordinates to Rani."

"Will do."

Cara put her headset down on the desk and looked at Ferrero. "Can you notify the rest of Mamba for me, please?"

He grinned at her. "Welcome to the jungle."

Once he was gone, Thurston said to Cara, "I notice you didn't send Reaper out."

Cara shook her head. "I don't think we're finished with this thing in Cameroon. I've been doing some digging into Rassie Markram. It seems that when he wants something, he takes it by any means necessary. Which includes backing coups. I can hazard a guess there is a diamond mine involved in Cameroon somewhere. And while we can't prove that he was behind the plane being shot down, we can assume he gave the order, because he was backing the other side."

"I did my own digging too," Thurston said. "He owns a fleet of cargo planes, C-130s, and the like."

"His men still control the airport in Douala. Meanwhile the rebels are starting to cleanse the country of people who support the wrong side." Cara leaned over a keyboard and tapped a few keys. A picture appeared on the big screen. "This is the man behind it all. Moumi Onana."

Thurston nodded. "Africa is slipping back in time. Once again foreign interests are changing governments in countries."

"I have a feeling that this is just the beginning. Now we could have terrorists operating as poachers too."

Thurston patted her on the shoulder. "Welcome to my world."

BOTSWANA/ZIMBABWE BORDER

Suma kneeled and picked up some of the damp earth and smelled it. She dropped it to the ground and turned her head to Kagiso, her second in command. "They are back across the border. An hour, no more."

She was talking about the poachers. They had come across a trail and found the damp earth where one of them had pissed. "Tabia, the radio."

A slim Black girl came up to them and squatted down so Suma could access the radio. "Mamba Three, from Scout One, over."

She waited for a moment before Ollie Smith came back. "Copy, Scout One."

"Mamba Three, we have just found a fresh trail. The poachers are back across the border, over. What do you want me to do?"

"Wait one, Suma."

There were a few moments of silence while Smith and Flint discussed what they wanted to do, then Smith came back, his voice crackling over the radio. "Scout One, copy?"

"Roger, Mamba Three."

"Suma, follow the new trail. See what they're up to. Do not engage unless you have to."

"Roger. Changing mission."

Suma called the squad together and designated her point people. Then they set out following the fresh trail. They followed it until dark when they moved off the trail and set up camp on a low hill among some large rocks to provide shelter for them. Suma posted lookouts and they settled in for the night.

Suma was shaken awake not long after midnight by Kagiso. "Suma, wake up."

"What is it?"

"There is gunfire."

Suma was awake now. She sat and listened but shook her head. All she could hear was the others sleeping. Kagiso said, "Come."

They moved beyond the edge of the camp so that they were clear of the camp noise and Suma listened again. Then she heard it. The rattle of automatic gunfire. "They are slaughtering a herd," Suma said through gritted teeth. "Get everyone up."

Within minutes the squad was moving single file toward the distant sound.

————

TED CLARKE SHOOK Roy Roberts awake. "What is it?"

"Suma and her ladies are moving."

Strike Team Mamba had settled in for the night with the rest of the anti-poaching patrol. After hitting the ground Roberts had put his task force on an intercepting track, but it sounded like that was all about to change.

"What's happening, Ted?"

"Sounds like the poachers they were tracking are slaughtering a herd. Automatic weapons."

"Fuck." Roberts climbed to his feet. "Wake up Bravo. Tell them we've got a situation."

"You think Suma will engage them?" Clarke asked.

Roberts grunted. "Of course she fucking will. Wouldn't you?"

"I guess I would."

CHAPTER 6

MOSEKI CAMP

Cara stumbled into the ops center to find Ferrero, Rani, and Kayla waiting for her. "What have we got?"

Ferrero pushed a cup of black coffee into her hand and said, "It looks like poachers are slaughtering a herd of elephants, and Suma is about to open a can on them."

Cara picked up her headset. "She was ordered not to engage."

"She is a stubborn one," Kayla said. "A fighter when it comes to the animals."

"These aren't ordinary poachers, Kayla," Cara pointed out.

"Suma isn't an ordinary officer," Kayla replied.

"I hope you're right. Talk to me, Rani."

"I'm trying to find a satellite to piggyback on but there is nothing."

"Get Slick out of bed," she said curtly.

"Yes, ma'am."

Cara said, "Mamba One, copy?"

"Roger, Bravo. Good morning, boss."

"If you say so. I need a sitrep."

"We're about four klicks from Suma's last known position. We've been trying to link up with her but she's not answering."

Cara glared at Kayla. The anti-poaching squad commander said, "I will speak to her when she returns."

"Keep going, Roy. We'll see if we can raise them."

"Yes, boss."

Then red-haired wonder, Sam "Slick" Swift appeared. "Talk about wake a guy from a great dream."

"Code again?" Cara asked.

He grinned at her. "Is there anything else?"

"I truly worry about you, Slick. Rani, give him coordinates. Slick, we need a satellite."

He cracked his knuckles. "Your wish is my command, boss."

A few keystrokes later and he said, "We're up."

Rani shook her head. "How do you do that shit?"

"I am one with the medium," he gloated.

"Find Suma and her girls, Slick," Cara said.

"Yes, ma'am."

———

BOTSWANA/ZIMBABWE BORDER

They found the first elephant just on dawn. Suma kneeled beside the giant beast and examined where the tusks had been removed. All around it the trampled grass was red, indicating that the magnificent animal had died hard.

Kagiso kneeled beside her. "They are close. The herd went east toward the border trying to get away."

"We will follow them."

"You know that the others have been trying to reach us on the radio."

Suma nodded. "I will talk to them after."

"Suma, we are all in this together."

She shook her head. "This is our land; these are our elephants. Move out."

Kagiso stared at her before saying into her comms, "Everybody move."

———

FERRERO LOOKED at the screen and said, "All right people, Papa Bear is on deck." It was one of his favorite call signs from the series *Hogan's Heroes*. "Get me a line to Mamba."

"You've got it, Luis," Swift said.

"Mamba One, copy?"

"Copy, Zero."

"Just to let you know the boss has stepped out of the office and everything comes through me now, over."

"Roger that."

"Sitrep?"

"Everything seems all right. You tell me."

"We're still not having any luck raising Suma and her squad. So—"

"Sir, you need to look at this," Rani said, interrupting. "They just appeared out of nowhere. They knew they were being followed."

She brought up a new picture on the big screen and right away, Ferrero could see what the problem was. "Who or what is that second group?"

"I don't know, sir, but the formation they're set out in screams ambush."

"Shit. Suma, come in, over."

No reply.

"Suma, answer damn it, you're walking into a fucking ambush."

Still no reply.

"Jesus Christ. Mamba One, we believe that Suma and her girls are about to walk into an ambush. Pick up the pace, over."

"Copy, Zero. Picking up the pace. Out."

Ferrero went back to the screen and snapped, "Slick get me a real-time fucking feed on that position."

But it was too late. The scouting team walked into the ambush and the first girl fell. Ferrero stared at the screen. "Good grief."

———

TED CLARKE WAS on point and moving fast when the first reports from gunshots rolled across the landscape. At first it was a long burst of automatic gunfire which eventually settled down to well-placed shots.

Almost instantly his comms lit up with cries for help and warnings from squad members. There was no use trying to talk, instead, Clarke changed channels. "Roy, copy?"

Clarke's voice jumped around as he ran.

He got nothing back.

The shooting got louder, and Clarke suddenly stopped. "Fuck," he hissed when in front of him he found the first of the dead girls. He leaned down to check her. She was still warm but unresponsive. "Mamba One, copy?"

"Copy, Two."

"I've got a girl down. KIA. Moving toward the sound of the guns, over."

"Hold position, Ted. We'll be with you directly."

"Copy."

Clarke remained in position as he listened to the gunfire which was lessening with each minute that ticked by. Roberts and the others came out of the long grass and the Mamba leader crouched beside his second. He looked at the dead girl and shook his head.

"They fucking walked right into it," Clarke said.

"Right. Take Ollie and the second squad and circle around to the left. I'll take the others and go right. We'll out flank them and hit them from both sides."

"What about the girls?"

"I'm not sending my people into the trap they just fucking walked into. Go."

Clarke took his team and circled around, trying to resist the urge to go in hard and get his team slaughtered. Ollie said, "I think we're almost there."

The gunfire was sporadic now, a single shot here and there. "Fuck," Clarke hissed.

"Mamba One, copy?"

"Copy."

"We're too late. You hear that firing?"

"Yes."

"They're shooting the wounded."

"Understood," came the reply. "Hold position."

"What the fuck?"

"I said hold."

"Copy."

A few heartbeats later he heard Roberts say, "Bravo One, copy?"

"Read you loud and clear, Mamba One."

"I believe that they are shooting the wounded to draw us in. Can you confirm?"

"Confirm your last."

"We need a heli on site. Am holding position until morning, over."

"Mamba One, this is Bravo. Copy your last, I'll see what I can do. Out."

Clarke sat in the morning sunlight, hidden in the grass, and listened as the sounds of the murdering continued.

———

ROBERTS CLOSED Suma's sightless eyes and stood erect. Everywhere around him the dry, straw-colored grass was blotched with dried blood. He had Clarke and Ollie Smith doing a body count, but he was reasonably sure that they were all dead.

The poachers had made sure of that. They had stripped the women of their clothes and taken all their weapons and equipment. In the distance, Roberts could hear the noise of the Chinook helicopter coming toward them.

Clarke appeared at his side and said, "We're one short."

"Who?"

"Kagiso."

Roberts nodded. "Grab Taja and scout around. See if they've taken her. I'll give you a couple of hours."

"Copy, boss."

Clarke disappeared and Roberts said into his comms. "Zero, copy?"

"Copy. Sitrep."

"They're all dead except for one MIA. I have a man looking for her now."

"Roger. Keep me updated, Roy."

"Yes, sir."

Across the other side of the killing zone, Clarke found Taja. She was a thin girl, sinewy, wire tough, short hair. "Taja?"

She looked at the Brit and he could see the tears in her eyes as she wept for her friends. "I'm sorry, Mr. Ted."

"It's all right, girl. Listen. Kagiso is missing. We're going to see if we can find her."

Taja nodded. "Yes, okay."

"Is your ammo and water good?"

She held up her M6. "I am good."

"Fuck it, hang on. Simon, over here."

"What's up?"

"Change weapons with Taja."

"What?"

"We're going to look for Kagiso. Give her your 417, mate."

Flint was about to protest then said, "Fuck it."

"They swapped the weapons and ammo and Taja said, 'Thank you, Mr. Simon.'"

"Don't forget to duck," he replied.

They left the massacre site and trekked east toward the border. An hour later, they were within sight of it. "They have gone across."

"Yes," Clarke replied.

Taja looked around the ground at the trail they had been following. She paused and squatted. "Here, Mr. Ted."

Ted looked where she was pointing. "What am I looking at?"

She traced the faint outline of a boot with her finger. "See. Kagiso is following them. Not far away."

"How do you know she is following them?"

"Her steps are lighter than if she was a prisoner."

Clarke looked at the landscape ahead of him. "We can't go any further, Taja. We're not cleared to cross the border."

"What about Kagiso?"

"She's a smart girl. We'll have to rely on her to find her way back to us."

"Yes, Mr. Ted."

"I'm sorry."

"Me too."

An hour later they were back at the massacre site. "She's alive, boss, but by now she's across the border."

Roberts nodded. "You made the right call. Let's head back. Get on the heli."

———

MOSEKI CAMP

"What's happening?" Kane asked Cara as he entered her office.

She looked up at him and sighed. "One shit storm after another. I need you to prep the team to go back into Cameroon."

"Seriously?"

She nodded slowly. "You've been tasked to go after Moumi Onana. He is Omossola's right-hand man on the ground. Find him, kill him, get out."

"It's a fucking war zone."

"Yes, it is."

"Are these your orders?"

Cara nodded. "I'm giving them."

"Fine."

"Listen, Reaper, this is hard enough without blow-back from you. This mission is important, but it won't be the only one. The British government wants us involved in Cameroon."

"What about the strike teams?"

"Mamba is off chasing poachers who killed our people. The other teams are busy. You're it."

"We're one short," Kane pointed out.

"I know that, but you'll be fine this trip. Next trip we'll see about getting you a new shooter."

"What about Kayla?"

"She has a kid and Knocker is sleeping with her."

"All right, but I think she would fit."

"Get Knocker to stop shagging her and I'll think about it. Just while we're in Africa."

"I'll have a word with him."

"Fine. I'll have Luis gather all the intel you'll need, and you work the problem. You leave tonight."

THE TEAM GATHERED around the table and watched Kane put down the intel packets. "We've got a mission."

"Where we going?" Knocker asked.

"Cameroon."

"It sodding would be," the Brit growled.

"Study the intel and memorize what you can about the target."

Brick looked up. "Target?"

"Moumi Onana. Our mission is to give him a very bad day."

"This sounds fucked up already."

Kane unfurled the map Ferrero had supplied. "This

is the area he's operating at the moment. There's a small village at the center and I have no idea how to pronounce the name. We'll just call it Dodge."

"Man, I wish Cara was here."

"Well, she's not. Heads in the game."

They talked and thought and looked and thought some more until they came up with a plan. Knocker said, "I don't like the drop zone. I know beggars can't be choosers, but I still don't like it."

Kane nodded. He looked at the circled areas on the map which indicated rebel hotspots. Somehow they would have to go right through them. "No choice."

"We can still drop on the village."

Kane shook his head. "No, we overshoot and we're in the river and become a croc snack. We drop short and the rebels pick us up. Drop on top and we're in St. Mere Eglise in World War Two."

"Fine, it was worth a try."

"We'll take extra ammo, frags, and claymores. Expect to pack heavy. Go light on the MREs. I expect to be on the ground twenty-four hours, forty-eight tops."

"What about extract?"

"Helicopter at an LZ across the river."

"How the hell do we get across that?"

"Village on the river, will most likely have a boat."

"Just the four of us?" Brick said.

Kane nodded. "That's right."

"What about air support?" Knocker asked.

"Don't count on it. We'll take our own."

They looked at him as though he was crazy. "What have you been smoking?" Knocker asked.

Kane grinned. "Over here."

They followed him and he picked up a suitcase sized container. He opened it and exposed what was within. "This, people, is the AMX-4, codenamed Rhino. It is a quadcopter platform which mounts a small four-barreled rotary machine gun that fires a 5.56 bullet. It also carries a hundred round magazine like the M249. It arrived today."

"Where the hell did this beasty come from?" Lofty asked, trying to hide his excitement at the technology that would assist them.

"Global's scientific and arms manufacturing division," Kane explained. "Eventually we will all be trained to use it but at the moment, because he is the only one of us quad certified, Lofty, this is your baby."

Lofty's excitement waned and he didn't seem impressed at the prospect. "You mean I have to hump this through the jungle?"

"That's the other thing. It's able to be broken down and humped in a pack. Everything is lightweight but durable. We'll each carry one magazine for it. An extra four hundred rounds could make a difference where we're going."

"If it's for making life easier, I'm for it," Knocker said. "We can always divvy up the extra load."

Kane nodded. "Great. The good news is the tech heads are working on new stuff all the time so we can expect more special equipment as we go along."

"Do we know what's happening with Mamba?" Brick asked.

"They're RTB with one still in the field. The poachers carved the anti-poaching squads up something fierce."

"Losses?"

"Too many, including Suma."

"Fuck."

"Mamba will get them."

"Who is in the field?" Knocker asked.

"Kagiso."

"What the fuck is the girl doing?"

"She's following the poachers. They have prisoners," Kane told them. "They've headed into Zimbabwe."

"I hope she's okay."

"Me too."

———

ZIMBABWE

Kagiso moved like a feline through the long grass. Silent, stealthy, deadly. She crept forward pushing the dry grass carefully aside with her hands so she could get a better look at the village.

She moved like the lion currently out in the grass stalking her. Yet she kept her cool to achieve what she had to accomplish. She still had her M6 and most of her full complement of ammunition.

The lion had been stalking her for the past half hour, even in the daylight. Kagiso guessed it was attracted to the poachers' camp by the stench and the smell of fresh meat from the Impala that had been killed and left hanging.

She had caught sight of the animal once, the tawny colored fur almost the same color as the grass it traveled through. Kagiso knew she would be too exposed there in the open, even with her camouflage. She would circle around to the trees and bushes on the other side of the camp and out of the wind where hopefully the lion would lose her and concentrate on the carcass that was hanging from the frame on the edge of the camp.

Moving through the long grass, Kagiso made sure

she drew no undue attention to herself. It took thirty painstaking minutes of slow movements to reach her goal. Finally, she found a place where she could observe the camp and learn things.

She'd been in place for twenty minutes when a twig broke behind her. She spun around, immediately feeling the blood in her veins turn to ice. Standing there staring at her was the lioness that had been stalking her.

As Kagiso contemplated what to do, she said in a low voice, "You don't want me, mama. Go back to your babies."

The lioness sat down, showing off her swollen nipples. Kagiso guessed that her cubs weren't very old and had to be hidden in the long grass somewhere close by. "Go on, mama, your babies are waiting for you."

The lioness huffed and rose to her paws before turning away and disappearing. Kagiso felt a surge of relief the big cat hadn't attacked her, and she hadn't been forced to kill it.

Voices drew Kagiso's attention back to the camp. They were growing louder as two of the poachers walked and smoked. She could hear their words clearly and frowned. This was not at all what she had expected. These were no ordinary poachers. It was possible that they belonged to Boko or the new terror outfit on the block, United African Liberation Front. She thought maybe the second.

Waiting there a long time before deciding she'd heard enough, Kagiso was certain they were the ones responsible for the massacre of her people and were holding prisoners on site. Now it was time for her to get away to call in some help. If only she had the comms unit that Suma insisted they discard.

It wasn't until she was about to move that the barrel

of a weapon pressed against the side of her head. "What do we have here?"

———

KAGISO WAS STRIPPED of her weapons and shoved into a grass hut where she was placed under armed guard. Part of her training under Team Reaper had been to take stock of your surroundings in all circumstances. With that in mind, she'd counted at least thirty terrorists and multiple buildings. One of which had a radio aerial attached to a tree to keep it camouflaged.

Most of her captors were armed with AK-47s and handguns. Many of the younger ones wore baseball caps. The one thing that stood out to Kagiso was that there were very few women in camp. Those that were there did chores and walked around with faces covered and heads bowed in subservience.

Kagiso had been shut away for three hours before they came for her. She was carried and dragged to a large mud hut in the center of the camp. At first, she struggled. Her captors beat her with rifle butts until she stopped. Getting out alive would require all her strength. If they kept beating her, she would lose that edge and die here.

She stood in front of their leader. A narrow-eyed man who hid his face behind a mask. Despite that she could tell he was white. Behind him was a UALF flag. It was green and orange.

"Who are you?" he asked with a deep guttural voice. The man was undoubtedly South African. The question was, what was he doing here?

"I am Kagiso," Kagiso replied. There was no point in lying, it would only give them cause to torture her.

"Why are you here?"

"I am following poachers."

The leader glanced at a second man standing beside him. This one was African. The leader said nothing to him, just turned his attention back to Kagiso. "You are following poachers?"

"Yes, they killed my friends, so I followed them. They led me here."

"You are part of the anti-poaching squad at Chobe?"

"Yes."

"Was anyone else with you?"

"No."

The leader looked at the second man again. "We found nothing. The only weapons were those she had on her. No radio or anything else."

"Take her back to the hut," the leader said. "I will decide what to do with her after the ivory shipment has been taken."

"We should just kill her," the second man said.

"I will decide when."

"Yes, sir."

———

THEY SHOVED Kagiso into a hut and slammed the door. She climbed to her feet and quietly crossed back to the door she just entered. Through a crack in it she saw the guard outside.

She had until the following day. It was all the time she needed. Reaching down into her boot she found the small capsule shaped device. Taking it out she turned the top half a quarter turn. Immediately it started to flash red.

Satisfied, Kagiso walked back across the single room hut and sat down, pressing her back against the wall. Now all she had to do was wait.

———

MOSEKI CAMP

"Kagiso's tracker just came online," Ferrero said to Cara. "About three minutes ago."

The trackers were experimental units provided by Global. They had been handed out to the anti-poaching teams after Knocker and Kayla had disappeared. They were trackers and distress beacons wrapped up in one.

Cara nodded. "It's good to know they work. Where is she?"

"Zimbabwe. A few miles across the border."

"Get Mamba up. I want them airborne in twenty minutes."

"Into Zimbabwe?"

"No, they cross the border on foot. Have the helicopter remain on site for extract. Send Taja and her team with them. They will act as security for the helicopter. They are not to cross the border with Mamba. Understood?"

"Yes, ma'am."

"Bring her home, Luis."

CHAPTER 7

"Zero, this is Reaper One. Radio check, over," Kane said in a low voice.

"Copy, Reaper One, read you Lima Charlie, over." It was Rani.

"What's going on, Bravo One?"

"Zero is tied up with something so you are stuck with my sexy voice, over."

"Copy. All Reaper elements are on the ground and ready to move, over."

"Roger that."

Kane turned to the others. Himself, Lofty, and Brick were carrying M6s. Knocker had jumped with a Heckler and Koch 417. Even though it was a designated marksman weapon, it was still good for work in the jungle.

The team had jumped from the experimental Co-32, a new plane derived from the Concorde which had stealth capabilities. Now they were on the ground and ready to move.

"Bravo One, copy?" Kane said.

"Copy, Reaper One."

"How is ISR looking?"

"You've got a camp to your south and another to the east. If you head north for two klicks and then track east, you should be in the clear."

"Anything on Onana?"

"Nothing as yet. Keep the village as your target."

"Copy. Reaper One out." Kane looked at Knocker. "Up front, old chap. Brick, rear security. Let's move."

Knocker took them out on their northerly bearing. Once he figured they'd gone two klicks at snail's pace he turned them east. "Bravo One, copy?"

"Copy, Reaper Two."

"We're making the turn. How are we looking?"

"All clear for the next few klicks, Reaper Two," Rani replied. "I'll let you know if ISR picks up anything."

"Copy. Out."

After two more kilometers of tracking through the jungle, Kane called a halt. They looked over their map and worked out there was still at least a couple of kilometers to go until the next waypoint. There they would turn again to avoid what appeared to be another rebel camp before tracking through the village where, hopefully, Onana was located. It was far from perfect, but what mission ever was?

In all, it looked that there were maybe a thousand rebel forces spread throughout the Sud. In particular, the part where Reaper team were now patrolling.

Knocker kept them moving forward until Rani

interrupted the silence in his ear. "Reaper Two, hold position."

Knocker went to ground. "Copy, Bravo One. Sitrep."

"You've got what looks to be a rebel patrol headed your way. Maybe ten to twelve combatants strung out along the trail. About five minutes out."

"Copy. Break. Reaper, you get that?"

"Roger. Head into the jungle and hold position, Two. We'll do the same."

"Copy."

Knocker gripped his 417 and slipped into the dense, damp foliage. Soon he was out of sight, cloaked in the jungle's protective darkness.

The Brit waited in silence for the first rebel to appear. The sounds of the jungle were the indicators of the additional presence. The night creatures went silent. Then a dark shadow emerged out of the gloom followed by another.

They reached where Knocker was hiding and stopped. The Brit grew tense almost certain that they must have sensed him. Then he heard a voice say in French, "Damn insects are eating me alive."

"Bug repellent isn't worth shit," said the other.

"Piss on your hands and wipe it on yourself," said Knocker.

The men spun around bringing their weapons up.

"Hold it, chaps, I'm friendly."

"Who are you?" one of them asked, his weapon not wavering.

"Raymond Jensen, former SAS, now working for Global as part of Team Reaper. You blokes legionaries?"

"Yes."

"Good. Reaper, these guys are French."

"Copy. On our way."

———

COMMANDANT THEO GIROUD crouched beside Kane and said in a low voice, "We ran across some rebels at dusk and were in a firefight. We got away but cannot be extracted until morning."

"How many men do you have?"

"Fifteen."

Kane said into his comms. "Bravo One, I need intel on the rebel groups' current locations."

"Reaper, they are holding in a defensive position at the moment."

"The village?"

"No movement."

"No movement as in no movement?" Kane asked.

"Affirmative."

"That's not right."

"Roger that."

"We're headed for the village too," Kane told him about their mission. "Seems we're headed in the same direction."

The Frenchman nodded. "Shall we continue?"

"Yes."

They moved out into the darkness and more by good luck than anything else, they reached the village and the mission. "Giroud, we need a perimeter," Kane said.

The Frenchman nodded. He turned to one of his men and said, "Sergeant, see to it."

Kane turned to Knocker. "Work with the sergeant."

"Roger that."

"Now, Commandant, shall we go and find our target?"

———

Onana sat staring into the fire, wrecking his night vision capabilities. From the darkness came his radio operator, a tall, willowy man whose skin was as dark as the night from which he emerged.

"Colonel?"

Onana looked up. "Yes?"

"The French are making for the village."

"I see. If they expect to find me there, they are sadly mistaken."

"That is not all. There are reports that another team of mercenaries have appeared and are making for it as well."

"What mercenaries?"

"We do not know."

The rebel commander sighed. "It is a mess, Pierre. We wanted to take back control of our country but all we have done is invited the French, the South Africans, and most probably the British into our country. It will be a fight we cannot win."

"Then what do we do?" Pierre asked.

Onana got to his feet. "We fight, Pierre. We fight."

———

DOUALA INTERNATIONAL AIRPORT, CAMEROON

Markram stepped down from the plane and walked across the tarmac to where Galloway awaited him. The mercenary saluted his boss and said, "To what do we owe the pleasure, sir?"

"There was an emergency meeting at the UN a few hours ago in which the British were cleared to put troops on the ground as a security force for their diamond mines."

Galloway nodded slowly. He knew what it meant. The British owned three of the largest diamond mines in the country. Markram's end game once Omossola was in power. He wanted those mines. What's more, he needed them.

Galloway said, "What do you propose?"

"I want small strike teams sent out to take over each of the mines before the British can get their security forces in there. They are sending airborne troops, which means you have less than six hours to get it done."

"That is cutting it fine, sir. How long do you want them held?"

"Until Omossola can get enough troops in the area to force the British to withdraw."

Galloway looked perplexed. "Sir, what we need is a battalion. And that is for just one mine site."

"That is why I got you some help." Markram turned and looked back at the man coming down the steps from the private jet.

Galloway shook his head. The devil had come to Cameroon.

———

THE SUD

"Reaper One, you have approximately two hundred rebel troops closing in on your position from the north, more from the south. It looks like they're trying to cut you off."

Kane looked at Giroud. "We have incoming."

"I'll get my men ready."

"Knocker, things are about to get nasty."

"Roger that. It wouldn't be natural to have it any other way."

They had arrived at the village and found it deserted. Which meant their target wasn't there and now they were in the middle of a spider's web of rebels.

"Knocker, find a good defensive position and prepare for contact. Lofty, is the Rhino ready?"

"Roger that."

"Be prepared."

"Reaper One, this is Bravo One. The rebels have stopped. Unsure at this time—"

The howl of incoming mortar rounds drowned out the rest of the transmission. Explosions rocked the village and huts began to burn. This was just a taste of things to come.

———

KNOCKER OPENED fire as the handful of rebel fighters came out of the darkness and entered the circle of light thrown by the burning hut. If the rebel mortar attack had done one good thing, it was illuminating the battleground.

The lead attacker flailed as he fell to the hard-packed ground. Behind him, the others came on and Knocker changed targets. Another burst from the 417 and another fell. He grabbed for a grenade and pulled the pin. He threw it out and moments later it detonated, sending the other rebels to their deaths.

Movement to his left caused him to swing around. He was about to fire when he saw it was one of the French fighters. "Damn it, Marius, what the fuck are you doing?"

"The commandant said you might need some help over here."

The Brit nodded at the man's Heckler and Koch 416. "Can you use that?"

Marius glared at him. "Fuck you."

Knocker grinned. "You'll do."

"Reaper Two, copy?"

"Roger."

"I need you to move to the south side of the village. Lofty is waiting there for you. The rebels are about to mount a major push there."

"Copy, on my way."

Knocker slapped Marius on the shoulder. "Hold the line, Frenchy."

Then he was gone.

As he ran through the village, he couldn't help but see the devastation. Fires destroyed buildings which had once been homes. Most of what the rebels had thrown at them for the past thirty minutes were probing attacks. The assault from the south would be their first full on push. And boy, were they in for a surprise.

Knocker dropped down beside Lofty who crouched behind a mud brick wall. "What's up, Mucker?"

"Rani says these pricks are going to hit us hard through here."

"Perhaps we should show them the error of their ways."

Out of the darkness Kane appeared, and with him was Giroud.

Knocker said, "Didn't think we could handle it?"

"Didn't want to miss the show."

The Brit grinned. "Typical, want to hog all the glory for yourself."

The night was ripped apart by incoming mortar rounds before Kane could reply. The four men hunkered down behind the wall and waited while the night was shattered all around them. Dirt and debris rained down upon them as they waited patiently.

Then just as it had started, it abruptly stopped.

"Here they come," said Kane. "Lofty, get the Rhino up."

With a high-pitched whirring sound, the Rhino lifted into the air and showed the enemy just how devastating it could be.

A line of ten rebels emerged from the darkness, shouting and shooting. Their bullets hammered into the wall the team members were sheltered behind. Unflinching, Kane, Knocker, and Giroud opened fire, picking their targets.

More rebels appeared behind the first row, urging those in front of them along. Knocker shouted, "Are you going to fucking join in anytime soon?"

"Just as soon as I find the fire button," Lofty replied.

"You have got to be shitting me. Everyone knows it's the fucking X button."

Above them, the Rhino came to life with devastating effect.

The rebels were mown down by the minigun as though they were tenpins. Kane and the others watched on in awe at the display.

The firing petered out and the whirr of the Rhino could be heard overhead. However, the ebb in the fighting lasted only a few more heartbeats as more rebels came charging out of the darkened jungle.

Again, the Rhino came to life as though a buzzsaw. The rebels were cut down like those before them. Then when the attack stopped, thirty rebels had died and no more threw themselves against the southern defenses.

"That'll wreck your fucking day," Knocker said in a low voice.

"You're right," Kane replied.

"Where did you get such a weapon?" the Frenchman asked.

"We have creative friends."

Kane heard Brick in his ear. "Reaper, we've got movement to the west."

"On my way, Brick. Bravo One, sitrep?"

Rani's voice came back to him. "Looks like the northern force has split. They're going to hit from two directions."

"Copy," Kane replied. He turned to the others. "Giroud, you want the north?"

"I will secure it."

"Lofty, go with him. Knocker and I will join Brick. Let's move."

———

ONANA LOOKED at his men as they staggered back into the camp behind the assault lines. They had been torn apart by a machine like nothing he'd ever seen before. He looked at one of his captains. "Is the next wave ready?"

"Yes, sir."

"Make sure they attack at the same time."

"Yes, sir."

He had two assault teams of thirty men. His aim was to overwhelm the numerically inferior force, but now the new weapon that they were using left doubts in his mind.

More wounded came in and a young lieutenant staggered over to Onana, a bloodied bandage around head and leg. "Sir, they fight like the devil. It is almost impossible to break through."

"Nothing is impossible," the colonel replied. "They are intruders in our country. They must not be allowed to leave. Get some rest. We will finish this fight."

CHAPTER 8

MOSEKI CAMP, BOTSWANA

Cara looked at the big screen and took note of the red dots, each signifying a rebel soldier. Ferrero moved in beside her and said, "They're about to hit them from two sides."

"Does Reaper know?"

"Yes."

"Casualties?"

Ferrero shook his head. "Both them and the French have been lucky so far. Just one wounded, and by all accounts, it is just a scratch."

"Thank God for small mercies."

"There is more. We're getting intel all the time on the fluid situation in Cameroon. The British are sending airborne forces to secure their diamond mine investments."

"Is that all?" Cara asked, hoping that maybe the British would join forces with the French and start pushing the rebels back.

"No. This one is even more interesting. Slick, do you have it?"

A smaller window opened on the large screen and a picture of a man appeared.

Cara frowned. "Why do I feel I should know him?"

"Nikita Chernov."

"The mercenary leader they call the Devil?"

Ferrero nodded. "That's the one. He flew into Cameroon this evening along with Markram."

"Why?"

"I had Slick look around and see what he could find. Not long after they arrived, Markram split one of his battalions into three and they moved out. Headed north."

"Show me the sites of the British diamond mines?"

Moments later they were there, indicated by blue dots on the screen. Cara thought for a moment. "Omossola has always sworn that should he take power, the British rapists of his country would be thrown out. Markram is going after the mines before the British can secure them with their own forces."

"That's what I figure. But he doesn't have enough men to hold them against the British and French. He needs help."

"Chernov. But what does he bring to the partnership?" Cara asked.

"Air support. He has a large fleet of Sukhoi Su-27s."

"Where are they?"

"They were in Syria. However, they have left their airfields, and no one knows where they are."

"On their way to Cameroon?"

"Most likely. If they park them in the north..."

"The risk of a full-blown war escalates."

"And no one has the heart for that since Afghanistan," Ferrero said.

"Shit. We always figured Markram was in it for something. It looks like the diamond mines are it."

"Yes, ma'am."

"I'll let Mary know. Have Mamba deployed?"

Ferrero nodded. "They should be on the ground now and moving toward the border."

Cara said, "Keep me updated."

———

AN EXPLOSION FORCED the three operators down behind the small embankment they were using for cover. To their left, two of the legionaries continued firing at the incoming rebels. Kane reached for a fragmentation grenade and pulled the pin. "Frag out!"

The deadly slivers ripped through the soft flesh of the attackers. Knocker opened fire and shot a rebel who'd been stunned by the blast. On the other side of Kane, Brick fired methodically, taking down more targets.

Eventually the attack waned and then petered out. The firing stopped and Kane looked around. He knew they couldn't put up with much more. "Reaper Four, how is the ammo for the Rhino?"

"Down to one box mag, Reaper One."

Kane looked at Knocker and Brick. "We can't keep this up. We need to turn things to our advantage."

"You're going to suggest something stupid, aren't you?" said Knocker knowingly, having been through too many scrapes with him to think otherwise.

"When you say stupid do you mean like a small

raiding party to try and scatter them into the jungle?" Kane asked.

"Yes."

"Yes."

"I knew it. What crazy dick do you have in mind to lead such an expedition?"

Kane grinned. "They tell me the SAS are good at behind the lines work."

Knocker groaned. "I'll take a Frenchy with me; between us we might be able to conjure something."

————

LORD WELLINGTON DIAMOND MINE, CAMEROON

Sergeant Ollie Yates hated the darkness. Well, not actually the darkness, but more the things you couldn't see. Especially in Africa. On his last deployment to the country, his team had lost a man to a lion attack on a night much like the one that enveloped them now.

His team of ten Pathfinders were the advance party to the airborne element which were to arrive just after dawn at the airstrip to the east of the mine camp. Until then, he and the small group of mine security were on their own.

And the rebels were closing in.

"Going to be touch and go, Sarge," the young private said as he emerged from the shadows.

Yates nodded. "I'd rather be on the North York Moors, Billy."

"How long you been at this lark?"

"Two marriages."

"Shit."

"Yes."

The night birds and insects suddenly went silent, and Yates strained to listen why. Maybe a predator. Maybe—

THWAP! THWAP!

Both Yates's and Billy's heads snapped back, holes in the center giving each a third eye. They dropped to the ground and out of the darkness came two men. One was David Galloway, the other was a Russian, one of the mercenary snipers. They stooped and checked the Brits before Galloway said, "Move in. Spare no one."

Minutes later, the mine site and camp were echoing with the sound of gunfire.

———

MOSEKI CAMP, BOTSWANA

Cara desperately wanted sleep but there was too much happening that needed her attention. Her phone rang and a familiar voice said, "I knew you'd still be up."

"Twice in one night, Mary, to what do I owe the pleasure?"

Mary Thurston paused before she said, "I know you're stretched thin on the ground, but we've been asked to look into something else."

"Can it wait? I've got Reaper in the middle of a shit fight, and Mamba in Zimbabwe chasing possible terrorists."

"Afraid not, Cara. What teams do you have left?"

"Leopard and Cheetah. I need at least one for security."

"I appreciate that," Thurston said. "The Brits have lost contact with the Pathfinders at the Lord Wellington Diamond Mine. They were meant to put an airborne force on the ground in three hours, but this could change things. They want us to have a looksee."

"What's wrong with the SAS?"

"Between you and me, their available teams are deployed elsewhere in the country."

"Christ. I'll see what I can do."

"Just recon, Cara. Nothing else."

"Yes, ma'am."

She disconnected the call and then hit dial again. Moments later a man answered, his voice, layered with sleep. "Sayers."

"Get Cheetah up, Luke, I've got an urgent mission for you."

"Yes, ma'am."

————

THE SUD, CAMEROON

They slipped back into camp two hours after leaving. Knocker and the French Legionnaire who wasn't even French; he was Irish. Knocker called him, "Paddy."

They infiltrated the rebels and planted a line of explosives that would be detonated by the first one to explode. It was one that Knocker would trigger.

Kane said, "Once you detonate, we go. I've got a BA flight booked for twenty minutes over the river. Looks like Onana lives to fight another day."

"What about the crocs?"

"Got it sorted."

"Then there's no time like the present to do it," Knocker said, pointing to the thin line of light to the east.

Kane said into his comms. "Everyone to the river. When I say, Knocker, set the ball rolling."

"I can see it now," Knocker muttered. "Croc stew."

Minutes later they were gathered at the river. In his possession, Kane had some fragmentation grenades. "Everyone, get ready. Knocker, let her buck."

"What?"

"Blow the damn thing."

"Why didn't you just say so?"

"Knocker—"

Suddenly a chain of explosions ripped the dawn apart. If the Brit knew a lot about soldiering, he knew more about explosives. And right at that point, the rebels were finding out just how extensive that expertise was.

The next ones to go were the grenades into the water. These would be used to scare the crocodiles away, or at least confuse them. Once they had detonated, the defenders of the village started across.

Knocker was the last one out of the water. Kane said, "See, you're still in one piece."

"For the moment. I just hope one of them dick fishes hasn't got in somehow."

Kane chuckled. "It's called a Candiru and they're native to the Amazon."

"Whatever."

"Let's move. We have an extract to meet."

———

MOSEKI CAMP, BOTSWANA

"Reaper and the French are airborne and, on their way, out of Cameroon," Ferrero said. He stared at Cara. "Go get some sleep."

"We still have a team in the field, another about to deploy, and the mission was a fuckup," Cara pointed out.

"There's nothing you can do about it at the moment," Ferrero said. "I'll wake you if something happens. One thing Mary didn't do was wear herself down."

"What about you?"

"I had a nap earlier."

She looked at him skeptically. Then Cara sighed. "Fine, but you wake me if something happens."

"It's fine, Cara. Go."

Ferrero went back out to the operations room. "What do we have on this fine morning, Rani?"

"Mamba are closing in on their target, sir, and Cheetah will be on the ground shortly."

The former DEA man nodded. "Slick, do you have a minute?"

"Be right there."

Moments later he joined Ferrero and Rani. "I want you two to work together and get target packages for Moumi Onana, Ignatius Omossola, Chernov, and Rassie Markram."

Swift raised his eyebrows. "As in *'target'* target packages?"

"Yes."

Rani nodded. "We can do that."

"Good. Let me know when it's ready. Meanwhile, let's get Kagiso home."

CHAPTER 9

ZIMBABWE

Mamba held back for most of the day, waiting for dusk before closing on the village where the terrorists were holed up. They had observed from a lay-up position and now it was time. Roberts took them in close where they could see the campfires and the patrols. He looked at the satellite feed on his robust tablet and saw the weak signal still flashing from Kagiso's tracker.

Roberts put it in his pack and said to Ted Clarke, "We take the patrols first and then move in. You and Simon take the machine gun nest and hold it. Ollie and I will get Kagiso. If we tip them off too soon, we're in a world of pain. That machine gun will come in handy."

"Got it, boss."

The first patrol was taken a few minutes later. Two short bursts from suppressed weapons and they were down. Their bodies were then dragged into the shadows and the assaulters moved on.

Clarke and Flint used the shadows to move on the

machinegun post. Since they were already inside the village, they were able to take it quickly. They crept up behind the two men and used their suppressed SIG Sauer P226 handguns to finish them off. Next, they repositioned the weapon so that it covered the terrorist camp.

All that had to happen now was to get Kagiso.

————

THE KNIFE SLID between ribs and punctured the man's heart. He stiffened and then went limp in Roberts's arms. Beside him, the terrorist that Smith was taking care of did the same.

They hid the bodies in the darkness of the shadows and kept moving toward the hut where Kagiso was being held.

After stopping twice they eventually made their target. Outside, stood an armed terrorist cradling an AK.

Roberts tapped his partner on the shoulder and Smith fired. The guard dropped and the pair hurried forward.

Smith grabbed the dead man by the collar while Roberts entered the hut. "Kagiso? Are you here, girl?"

"I am here."

The Mamba team leader flicked on his flashlight, shining it on the young woman. "It is good to see you, girl. Come on, it's time to leave."

"No, we need to take them with us."

"Who?"

"The other prisoners and the one in command. He is white. A South African. It isn't right. I think the television crew caught something they weren't meant to see."

"Where are they?" Roberts asked.

"In the hut next to this one."

"What about the white guy?"

"There is a hut near the center of the village. He is in there."

The Mamba commander gave her his sidearm and some spare magazines. "Can you get the prisoners out?"

"Yes."

"We'll meet you on the north side of the village."

"Yes, sir."

"Mamba Two, copy?"

"Copy, One," Clarke replied. "Change of plan. Meet us in the center of the village. Out."

"Copy. Out."

Roberts and Smith used the shadows once more to reach their target area. He found Clarke and Flint waiting for him. He pointed to a hut adjacent to where they were. "Our target is in there."

"What target?"

"I guess we'll find that out. Hold here. Me and Smithy will go in."

"Where is Kagiso?"

"Getting the prisoners."

"What fucking prisoners?"

"Long story. Wait here."

"Don't take too long. It's only a matter of time."

Roberts and Smith crossed the open ground and entered the hut. Moments later there was a shout and the sound of gunfire.

"Shit," Clarke growled. "One, sitrep?"

"Wait one."

Moments later he appeared with Smith and the prisoner. "Let's get out of here."

Gunfire erupted from the darkness.

"Contact right," Flint snarled and opened fire.

More stabs of light joined the first and the firing intensified. The strike team started their withdrawal to the north. Roberts's comms lit up. "Mamba One, sitrep."

The voice belonged to Rani. He said, "We have prisoners and we're taking heavy fire. Exfil is to the north. We will not make the LZ. I repeat, we will not—"

CRACK!

"Not make the LZ."

"Copy. Give me a moment and I'll reroute your exfil chopper. Standby."

The team pushed out of the village, Clarke and Flint covering their retreat, and met Kagiso on the edge of the bush and long grass. Along the way she'd picked herself up an AK and spare ammunition. "Are you okay, girl?" Roberts asked.

"I am fine," she replied. "This is Ian and Lisa. They are what's left of the TV crew."

Roberts said, "We'll talk later. Right now, we need to get out of here. Kagiso, take them north. Ollie will go with you to keep an eye on our friend."

"Yes, sir."

"Keep me updated—"

"Mamba One, copy?"

"I'm here, Rani."

"Your extract is twenty mikes out. There is a clearing big enough for it one klick north of you. Can you make it?"

"We'll be there." He looked at the others. "Get moving."

"Simon's hit," Ted Clarke called out as he grabbed his friend and helped him to his feet.

"Is he okay?" Roberts shouted above the gunfire.

"I'm fine," Flint said between gritted teeth. "Got me in the fucking suit."

"Fall back." Roberts grabbed a fragmentation grenade and pulled the pin. "Frag out!"

The ensuing explosion rocked the night.

They dropped back into the bush, Clarke reloading as he went. The thick scrub enveloped them and concealed their retreat. They caught up with the others and worked their way to the LZ.

Once there, they set up a small defensive position and waited. Roberts went over to their prisoner and stared at him. "Who are you?"

"Fuck off."

It was only two words, but the thick South African accent was there. Roberts said, "You're not terrorists. Just well-organized poachers."

"If you say so."

"Who do you work for? Markram?"

The man's eyes flickered ever so slightly.

The Mamba leader nodded. "Uh-huh." He stepped away and said into his comms, "Bravo One, how far out is that evac?"

"Two mikes out."

"Copy."

Suddenly the bush to their front erupted with explosions and Clarke and Smith appeared. They were being chased by bullets and found cover just as shooters appeared in the tree line. "That pissed them off even more."

"How many out there?" Roberts asked as he opened fire with his M6. Two men fell.

"A handful less than what there were," Clarke replied. "Maybe fifteen or twenty. Big operation, boss."

"We have to hold them for another couple of minutes."

"No sweat."

For the next minute, they kept up a withering fire before the harsh sound of a helicopter passing overhead split the night. The door gunner opened fire and the poachers fell back into the trees. The firing stopped and Roberts turned to his second in command. "Get them ready. We're going home."

———

MOSEKI CAMP, BOTSWANA

It was Cara and Ferrero who ran the interrogation of their new prisoner. Once the team arrived back, the South African was put into a small cell and left there for twelve hours before they pulled him out. In the meantime, Markram and his new associate, Chernov, took over the other mines in the north of the country, putting a halt to the incoming British force.

However, Cheetah was on the ground at the Lord Wellington and relaying information back. Ferrero looked at the latest report and said, "Fifty men on the ground. A mix of Markram's men and Russian mercenaries. Plus helicopter gunships and anti-aircraft missiles. Not something you want to walk into."

"Don't forget the tanks," Cara said.

"How much longer do you want to leave Cheetah on the ground for?"

"Until I receive word on our next move," Cara replied. "How is Kagiso?"

Ferrero nodded. "She is fine."

"Do you think she would be a good fit for Reaper?"

"You're asking the wrong person. You need to ask Kane. It's his team."

Cara shook her head. "No, it's *my* team. What is your assessment of her?"

"She's good. Not as good as Kayla, and now that Suma is gone, she would be the next best. I was thinking about giving her her own team."

"Hold off on that."

"Yes, ma'am."

"Let's go and talk to our friend."

On the other side of the compound, they approached the cell block. The day was warm and the anti-poaching squads were training under the watchful eye of Pete Traynor. When they entered the interrogation room, the South African was under the watch of two armed guards. Both were from the anti-poaching squad. Cara dismissed them and turned her attention to the man sitting at the table. She just stared at him for a moment, taking him in. Then she started.

"I'm going to take a stab in the dark and say you work for Rassie Markram."

The man stared at her.

"Care to tell me your name?"

He kept staring.

Cara nodded slowly. "Let's try something else. You will go away for murder and poaching. That's just for a start. Now, a white guy in a Zimbabwe prison, that would be bad for you."

"I didn't kill anybody in Zimbabwe."

Cara cocked an eyebrow. "He speaks."

Ferrero went and stood in front of him. "What's your name?"

"Benny Goss."

"Are you a poacher, Benny Goss?"

"I am a hunter."

"And a murderer," Cara added.

He gave her a bitter stare. It was then she realized the man had issues with women in authority. She walked around behind him and gave him an open-handed slap across the back of his head. He lurched to his feet, but only as far as his chains would allow. "Fucking whore."

She slapped him again. "Sit down, you murderous swine."

Ferrero put a hand on Benny's shoulder and forced him back into his seat. "Calm down. Just answer the questions and we'll see what kind of deal we can give you."

That got his attention. "What deal?"

Cara stared at him. "Maybe a nice jail cell that's not in Africa."

"No jail."

"Oh, make no mistake, you're going to jail," Cara said coldly. "The where is up to you. Maybe Sierra Leone. I'm sure we can find a dark hole there somewhere."

The threat didn't seem to faze him.

Ferrero said, "Or you could disappear in Brazil. I hear they have quite shitty accommodations."

That rattled him. In Africa, Markram could help him, but South America was another story. Then as Ferrero and Cara turned to leave, he said, "Yes."

They turned around and stared at him.

"Yes, I work for Markram."

"Why is he poaching?" Cara asked. "The guy is worth billions."

"It's a short-term fix," Goss said.

"For what?" Ferrero asked.

"His diamond mine has dried up. He's losing money hand over fist."

Cara stared at Ferrero. "That explains Cameroon."

"He's throwing it all at the coup," Goss said. "If it fails, he's flat broke. The diamond mines are everything."

Cara had a thought. "What if he can't take them in operational order?"

Goss said, "He needs them that way. If he can't have them operational, they're useless."

Ferrero said, "I can see what you're getting at, Cara, but the UN won't allow an airstrike on foreign soil."

"Then we do it ourselves," Cara said.

"The Brits will have a foal. Everyone is being pulled out."

"I'll run it up the chain. Have Reaper and Leopard standby."

"Yes, ma'am."

Cara left the building and walked back to her office. She picked up the phone and made the call.

"Thurston."

"Mary, it's Cara."

"How's things?"

"You certainly threw me into the deep end."

"I wouldn't have done it if I didn't think you could handle it. What can I do for you?"

Cara explained the situation with Rassie Markram.

"What is your plan, Cara?" Thurston asked.

"I want to make the diamond mines inoperable. I need your permission to send in the strike teams and

Reaper to make it so. If it works, we can hit Markram hard. It takes money to put an army in the field."

"If I grant you permission, you'll have the Brits climbing the walls."

"If I don't do it then they'll never get back in there."

There was a long silence before, "No. I can't allow it, not yet. Pull everyone out."

Cara was disappointed but accepted the order. "Yes, ma'am."

"Is there anything else?"

"I sent Reaper after Onana, but the mission failed. Luis drew up target packages for other top players in Cameroon. I want to send Reaper after them when the time is right."

"Something like the SAS and Delta did in Iraq when the insurgency was on?"

"Yes."

"Shelve it until you hear from me."

"Yes, ma'am."

The call disconnected and Cara made one more. "Luis, we're off."

———

MOSEKI CAMP, BOTSWANA

Kane found Kagiso cleaning her new M6A2 in the anti-poaching squad barracks. She'd just finished putting it back together. He said, "Come with me."

His words were abrupt and his tone could easily have been misconstrued that one might think they had done something wrong. But Kagiso got to her feet and followed him, carrying her weapon.

They went over to the strike teams' barracks. Once

inside she found Knocker, Lofty, Brick, and Kayla waiting for her. Kagiso frowned. "What is happening?"

Kayla stared at her and then smiled. "I'm letting you go."

"What?"

Kane said, "Since Cara has been moved—"

"Kicked," said Knocker. "Definitely kicked."

The Team Reaper commander nodded. "Since she's been kicked up the chain, we're one person short. I want you to come onboard Reaper."

Kagiso looked confused. "Me? I am a woman."

"So was Cara last time I looked. It'll be a trial basis, but I'm sure you'll do fine. Be warned, if you accept, I expect your best, and with what we're facing at the moment there will be tough times ahead."

"Do I get to order Kayla around?"

The anti-poaching commander smiled. "Absolutely."

"Then I will do it."

Kayla's smile widened even further, and she wrapped her arms around Kagiso, whispering in her ear, "Make us proud."

"Here," Knocker said.

Kagiso looked at him and he tossed her a Synopra-thetic suit. He said, "A word of advice, don't get shot, the cure is worse than the damn disease."

"Brick will get you kitted out," Kane said. "He'll set you up with a weapon, SIG, body armor, comms. Anything else you need, just ask. You'll also get a pay rise. It's up to you to take care of your equipment."

"Yes, boss."

"My name isn't boss. It's John, Kane, or Reaper. If I give you an order, I expect it to be followed without question. However, it's a two-way street. If there is a better way of doing something I will listen and make my judgment. Your callsign will be Reaper Four. I'm One, Knocker is Two, Lofty is Three, Brick is Five. He's also our combat medic as you know. If he says you're sick, you better lie down."

"Yes, sir," Kagiso replied with a nod.

"All right, get yourself squared away."

Kagiso left with Brick and Kane turned to Kayla. "Am I making the right decision?"

"She will not let you down."

"I hope not."

———

KANE ENTERED Cara's office and found her studying a map on the wall with Henry Blake, Strike Team Leopard's commander. She turned and said, "Good, you're here. Let's get started."

"What's up?" Kane asked.

"I did have a mission for Reaper, Leopard, and Cheetah but that is now put on hold. Instead, we go back to anti-poaching duties. Mamba will stay here and act as security."

Kane nodded. "Fine with me."

Cara poked at the map. "The target is here near the Humboldt River."

Kane looked at her. "What? I have trouble with some pronunciations, it starts with H."

"What's the objective?" Kane asked.

"According to our bird in the cage, there is another poacher camp set up two miles from the river in Zimbabwe. Markram has been paying authorities there to look the other way while he sets up shop and runs operations across the border. Reaper will infiltrate the area and close them down."

"What about us?" Blake asked.

"I want you to take an anti-poaching team across the border into Madikwe."

"Madikwe?"

Madikwe was a small safari reserve in the north of South Africa. It was fully fenced, but that never stopped poachers. "That's right."

"What is in Madikwe?"

"You're going to babysit some black rhinos. Make sure you take supplies for a week. After that I'll swap you out with Cheetah and another team."

"Ma'am, if you don't mind me asking, what about Cameroon?"

Cara's face remained passive. "Cameroon is no longer our problem. Markram and his poaching is now the focus."

"Mind telling me why?" Kane asked.

"Markram is strapped for money which is why he's backing the coup and poaching ivory," Cara explained. "We shut that down, and we restrict his money flow. That makes him angry and hopefully he'll mess up somehow."

Kane nodded. "Okay."

Cara said, "You'll get everything you need in the morning. You go tomorrow night. There was one other thing. Nikita Chernov has troops on the ground in Cameroon. I think he's working with Markram. Hopefully he'll stay there," Cara explained.

"Great, Russian mercs."

"Don't worry, if he pops up, you'll get your chance to have a go at him. I promise."

Kane nodded. "Just so you know, Kagiso is now part of Reaper."

Cara nodded. "A good choice."

"I thought so. Anything else?"

"No."

"Then we'd better get ready."

———

CAMEROON

Nikita Chernov was a solidly built man in his forties who, at one stage in his life, had the ear of the Russian president. All of that changed when he started his own mercenary business and got bigger than he should have. It was the way of the world. Private armies were the norm when it came to troops on the ground. Less pressure on governments that way.

However, Chernov looked confused. He turned to Markram and said, "I do not like it. My sources inside the UN are telling me nothing."

Markram nodded. "It's like a blanket of silence. However, the French and the Brits are starting to withdraw the troops they have in the country."

"Why?" Chernov asked. "That is the question. Why?"

"Because they are up to something."

Both men turned and stared the big broad-shouldered man off to their left. Ignatius Omossola was a proud man who looked at home in his combat fatigues.

"Of course, they are up to something," Chernov snapped. "But what? There wasn't even a response when we took the diamond mines."

"Speaking of the mines," Markram said, "are they secure?"

"Of course, they are."

"Then I need to start production."

Omossola stared at the South African. "Why so fast?"

"Because I'm running out of money." The embarrassment of the situation was almost too much for Markram as his anger surged. "If I don't have money, you can say goodbye to your fucking rebellion. The only thing keeping me afloat is poaching."

"What are you saying?" Chernov asked icily.

"Don't worry, Nikita, you'll get your money."

"I hope so, Rassie, because if there is any indication that you will fail to pay, my men will be on the next plane out of this godforsaken country."

"I will pay you in diamonds, just as we agreed."

"Then I will stay loyal to the cause." *Until I'm not.* "What about the mercenaries from England?"

"I have a plan if you are up to it."

"Doing something is better than waiting for it to happen."

"Good."

Omossola's satellite phone rang. He answered it and then broke out into a excited, almost childish glee. He disconnected and turned to the other two men. "We have him. We have Dewar."

PART TWO

A REAPER STALKS
THE DARK

CHAPTER 10

MOSEKI CAMP, BOTSWANA

"That puts the cat among the pigeons," Kane said as he looked at the big screen.

"We continue as planned," Cara replied. "It doesn't affect what we do. The UN has stated they will not recognize the illegal government."

"But they're still not sending in more troops, either."

"No. They're going to withdraw them. The African Union is going to—"

"Do nothing," Kane said, cutting her off.

"They have said they will suspend Cameroon from the Union and look at using peacekeepers if they can."

"We're going to need all the support we can get," Kane pointed out. "Just in case they decide to turn on us."

She nodded. "I talked to Mary, and she is deploying air support and a QRF team to forward areas where they can be useful."

"That's something, I guess," Kane replied. "What about here?"

"We still have Mamba for security. Plus, the anti-poaching squads. We'll keep deploying them."

"The move?"

"On hold."

Kane nodded. His expression softened. "How's everything else?"

"It sucks," Cara replied, letting her façade fall for just a moment.

"Command always was," he said.

"All I seem to be doing is losing people."

"Comes with the job," Kane said.

"If I give you an order, will you follow it?"

Kane was a little surprised by the question. "Don't I always?"

"Then before you leave, take me to bed."

"Now, that's an order I'll never disobey."

———

TARGET H, ZIMBABWE

"All Reaper elements on the ground, proceeding to target," Kane said over his comms. "Knocker, you're on point. Watch out a lion doesn't eat you."

As though on cue, a deep-throated roar sounded from somewhere in the distance.

"Great," said Knocker. "Lion supper coming up."

They started toward the poachers' camp. Intel had the numbers at around ten, so hopefully it would be an easy operation. They had dropped two miles from the target and would approach on foot.

Brick brought up the rear with Kagiso in front of

him. They walked single file, taking deliberate steps, trying to not make noise. A hundred meters from the target, Kane stopped them. "Kagiso and Knocker circle the camp and block squirters. We'll give you ten mikes to get into position. Go."

The pair disappeared into the dark. Kane said, "Bravo One, I need a real-time update."

"Copy, Reaper One. There are four roving patrols, and the rest looks reasonably quiet."

"Roving patrols?"

"That's right."

Kane frowned. "Are they walking set patterns or random?"

"Wait one."

"What's up, Reaper?" Brick asked.

"I have a bad feeling."

Brick nodded. He knew what that meant. "Knocker, hold position. The boss has a feeling."

"Ah bollocks. Holding."

"Reaper One, from Bravo."

"Go ahead."

"I've checked surveillance logs. These guys are walking set patterns."

"Like military?"

"Affirmative."

"Slick, you with me, buddy?"

"Copy, Reaper."

"Scan for any radio traffic or signals."

"On it."

"What's the issue, Reaper One?" Ferrero asked.

"Maybe I'm being too cautious, or we're walking into a trap, Luis. Just like Hyena did."

"Shit."

Kane brought his weapon up and swept the area.

He could see nothing. No movement out of the ordinary except for a guard. "Knocker, fall back on us."

"Copy."

"Rani, talk to me."

"Reaper, nothing has changed. They're just—wait."

"What is it?"

"Reaper, I've got a low frequency signal and I'm picking up Russian chatter," Swift said.

"Luis, we're going to need a hot extract now."

"Reaper, get down!"

The urgency in Rani's voice was unmistakable. Even so, it wasn't enough, for the night came alive with gunfire and tracer. And even as Kane went down, hit by two rounds, he heard Ferrero say, "Jesus Christ."

———

MOSEKI CAMP

Rani looked on in horror as the night came alive. Contacts sprang up everywhere as if by magic. Flashes of gunfire were followed by explosions. From across the ops room, she heard Ferrero say, "Slick, get a QRF team to that location now. We'll be lucky if we get any of them out alive."

"They're everywhere," Rani said. "It's like Hyena. Reaper One is down. Five is returning fire. Damn, Three is down."

"What about Two and Four?"

"They look to be taking heavy fire."

"Do we have anything in the area?"

Rani shook her head. "Nothing. What do we do?"

"Fuck." Ferrero thought for a moment before saying, "Nothing."

TARGET H, ZIMBABWE

Kane felt as though he'd been kicked in his chest. Everything screamed ambush even though he wasn't quite with it. In his ear through his comms he could hear Knocker growling at him. "You'd better fucking answer me, Reaper, or I'm going to be pissed."

Kane rolled onto his back, and he saw a tracer round streak across the sky. His NVGs had been dislodged, so everything was black. A shadow loomed up in front of him. His instincts told him that whoever it was, wasn't friendly. He pulled his SIG and blew off three shots. A high-pitched scream was followed by a dull thud. Kane moaned and said, "Someone talk to me. What the fuck is going on?"

"We're in the shit, mate," Knocker replied. "Walked right fucking into it."

"Everyone check-in."

"Two okay."

"Four okay."

"Five okay."

"One okay," Kane added. Then, "Lofty, check-in."

Nothing.

Bullets cracked close.

"Three, check-in."

Nothing.

"I have no response from Three. Five, can you see him?"

"All I can see is grass, Reaper. I'm pinned down."

"Bravo One, can you get a fix on Three?"

"He's lying in the grass to your left. Ten meters," Rani replied.

"Any movement?"

"Negative."

"Copy," Kane replied as he grabbed his assault rifle and started to crawl through the grass. All around them, Russian voices could be heard shouting through the gunfire.

Stalks of the stuff lay over onto Kane's back as a burst of fire scythed through the brown stalks. "Christ. Brick, can you get a grenade away?"

"Working on it."

A few moments later an explosion from a fragmentation grenade rocked the night. Kane found Lofty lying flat on his back, snoring softly. He'd taken a round to his ballistic helmet and had been knocked unconscious. "I've got Lofty. He's out like a light, took a round to his helmet."

"Kick the prick and wake him up," Knocker growled. "Fuck, that was close."

"Kagiso, how are you doing?" Kane said as he lay beside his fallen man.

"I'm scared."

"Me too. Just keep your head down. Zero, we need a way out of here before we all die."

"Working on it," Ferrero replied.

"Work faster."

"You know what this calls for, Reaper," Knocker said. "Some crazy sod to do something stupid."

"Oh, shit no."

"Oh, yes, it's Knocker time."

———

"WHAT ARE YOU DOING?" Kagiso asked Knocker.

The Brit had two grenades in his hands and his 417

was still attached by its strap. He used his teeth to pull the pins and looked at Kagiso. "This is what I do."

"Stupid things?"

"Aye, lass. Do you have any grenades?"

"One."

"Pop it."

"But—"

"Do it, before we all die."

Kagiso grabbed the grenade from her webbing, pulled the pin, and threw it. Then it exploded. "There, happy?"

"Hold on to your hat."

She watched in disbelief as Knocker came to his feet, bullets whipping all around him. Two clipped his clothing, tearing holes in the fabric. He threw the first grenade, then the second. Even before they had landed, he'd drawn his P226 and started firing at vague figures, shouting at the top of his voice.

———

MOSEKI CAMP

"No, no, no. No," Rani gasped as she watched what was happening through her ISR feed. "Dumb, stupid, bastard."

"What's happening?" Ferrero asked. He looked at the screen and saw the figure. "Damn it, Jensen."

They saw the explosions, the gunfire, the Russians falling. Knocker staggered but remained upright. They saw him holster his handgun and then reach for his 417. The Brit staggered again and then fell to his knees. He was hit by another round and toppled sideways.

Rani gasped. "Oh god no."

———

TARGET H, ZIMBABWE

The first bullet hurt like hell, the next two were killers. Just not literally. The Synoprathetic suit worked as it was supposed to, but it didn't stop Knocker from falling over in pain. "Fucking bollocks."

"Two is down, Two is down," the call came from Rani in the TOC.

"I'm fine," Knocker growled. "Just had—"

A figure appeared and pointed a weapon at the fallen operator. Knocker's 417 came up and roared to life. The Russian shooter staggered back and disappeared. There was movement behind the Brit, and he rolled over, ready to fire.

"It's me, *Ibhubesi*," Kagiso said using the Zulu word for lion.

"Good way to get yourself shot," Knocker snapped. He took the chance to reload. "Are you all right?"

"I am fine. I am scared, but still alive."

"Just keep shooting, luv. Just keep shooting."

———

KNOCKER WASN'T the only one who'd been shot multiple times. Kane had been shot twice, just thankful that the ballistic material they wore worked, and he hadn't been shot in the head. Brick also had been hit, but only once. Kane replaced an empty magazine with another and started to open fire again. Beside him, Lofty moaned. Then he made to sit up and would have had Kane not held him down. "Stay still. If you sit up, you'll lose your head."

"What happened?"

"You got shot. Now, stay down. Knocker, did that stunt work?"

"I don't think so. Bravo One, we need a sitrep on the situation."

"Still surrounded and under heavy fire. Does that answer your question?"

"I guess."

"Lofty, how are you feeling?"

"I'll live."

Kane thought for a moment. "Whoever has smoke left I want you to throw it toward the target. I don't care if it is dark. Copy?"

Smoke canisters went out and a curtain hung in the air. Then Kane looked at Lofty and said, "You ready?"

"Yeah."

"Everyone, throw grenades and pull back. Do it now."

Moments later explosions rocked the area and Team Reaper started to pull back, guided by Rani.

"Reaper, you have a shooter at your one o'clock."

"I can't see him."

"He's there."

Kane sprayed the long grass before him, and the shooter reared up. The target reeled away when Kane shot him. Moving forward Kane checked the fallen shooter. He was only wounded in the side.

He grabbed at his weapon and Kane kicked him in his wounded side.

A cry of pain and the man stared angrily up at Kane and cursed him in Russian.

"Who are you?" Kane asked in halting Russian.

The man spat at him.

Kane drew his P226 and placed it against the

wounded man's forehead just above the eye line. "Try again, buddy."

"Chernov."

One word was enough.

Kane hit him between the eyes and kept moving through the smoke.

They regrouped two hundred meters away from their starting point. Kane said to them, "We keep moving toward the border until Bravo can get us out. Just keep moving. Kagiso, you're on point."

"Reaper, what about Rhino?" Lofty asked.

"How long for you to get it put together?" Kane asked.

"A couple of minutes."

"Do it."

They set up a silent perimeter while Lofty got Rhino together. Once it was done, he said, "We're good to go."

Moments later the armed drone lifted, and the camera streamed live feedback to the control unit. The results were instant. They could see on the infrared feed the shooters coming up on them.

Kane said, "Knocker, you stay here with Lofty while he gives us some cover. The rest of us will move out. We'll set a direct course to the border. Just follow it."

"Copy."

As they moved away from the others, they could hear the rotary machine gun going to work.

———

MORNING SAW them in the clear. Knocker and Lofty had caught up, and there would be an extract come first light. Rani watched their backtrail and the Russians were nowhere to be seen.

"You figure that trap was set for us, Reaper?" Knocker asked.

"I'm guessing so."

"Then I guess it's time."

"Time for what?"

"Time to go balls to the wall and shut Markram down."

"That's the plan."

"I might know someone who could help."

"How?"

"He might have inside information into the smuggling scene."

"As in routes that are used to get them out of the country?" Kane asked.

"That's right. If Markram can't get them out, then that'll fuck things up for him. It might even prove more effective than getting shot at by poachers."

"I'll run it past Cara."

"Roger that."

The team was picked up an hour later by a Chinook. They were flown back to Moseki Camp where they were debriefed. With that done, Knocker and Kane approached Cara to discuss the proposal.

"Knocker knows a guy that might be able to help stop Markram getting his ivory out."

"Where is he?"

"Harare."

Cara thought for a moment. "Do it."

"Yes, ma'am."

CHAPTER 11

HARARE, ZIMBABWE

They drove a small yellow van around the packed streets of Harare, trying to look inconspicuous. The last thing they wanted was to draw attention to themselves especially with the turmoil that was running through the city at the time. With the death of Mugabe in 2017, a vacuum had opened which was filled by a man whose name was whispered by the public. Ngwenya—the Crocodile. His real name was Emerson Dambudzo Manangagwa or ED for short.

Things had come a long way since the days of farm invasions. With almost everything taken over, the whites were now leasing the land back and splitting profits with their owners. Well-tended fields growing maize, and tobacco drying sheds could now be seen.

However, there was still an element of violence toward foreigners on the streets. The small terror organizations that had been allowed to bubble below the surface.

"He has a bar up here," Knocker said to Kane and Kagiso.

"Cliché much?" Kane asked.

"It's where the money is."

"And you're sure that he will be able to point us in the right direction?"

"If he can't, he'll know someone who can. Ah, here it is."

The Brit pulled the Mitsubishi van over, grinding the gears. "Polishing the teeth?" Kane asked.

"Shut up, it's a piece of shit."

"You picked it," Kagiso said.

"Hey, you're the new chap. Keep your mouth shut."

"I'm not a chap. I'm a girl."

"Then keep your girly mouth shut."

Kagiso smiled. "You make it easy not to."

"I like her," Kane said.

"You keep your girly mouth shut too."

Knocker shut off the motor and looked at the front of the bar. Paint was peeling off the sign which boasted live music and dancing girls. Then there was the door. At one point in its life, it had been bright red. Now, from the sun beating on it, what was left of the paint was peeling and faded to a dull pink. Then there were the holes in the door itself.

"What kind of bar is this?" Kane asked.

"What it says. Live music and dancing girls."

"What about the bullet holes in the door?"

"The last time I talked to him, he was having some trouble with the local..." Knocker muttered something incoherent.

"What? Don't mumble."

"I said local crime figures."

"What crime figures?" Kane asked.

"ZUNA."

"Zimbabwe Ultranationalist Association?" Kane asked, thinking he might have misheard. "The terror organization?"

"That's right."

Kagiso shook her head. "Goodness me. Is your friend even still alive?"

"Of course he is. I think."

Kane checked his P226. "Kagiso, don't forget your gun."

"Yes, sir."

Climbing out of the van under the watchful gaze of some nearby bystanders, they walked across the sidewalk and into the club through the bullet-holed front door.

Inside it was dark and smelled of unwashed bodies and sweat. Somewhere among the cloying aroma was more than a hint of stale alcohol and cheap perfume. The music was being played from a stereo but the volume was low.

Knocker looked across at the bar and saw a man standing behind it, wiping a glass with a rag. When he walked over, the man smiled at him, showing stark white teeth against his dark skin. "Jesus Christ, mate, are you a fucking walking advertisement for White Bite or something?"

"What can I do for you, sir?"

"Is Johnny around?"

The man looked immediately on edge. "I'll have to check. Who are you?"

"An old friend. Ray from the Regiment."

"Would you like a beer while you wait?"

"Sure. Out of a bottle. None of the watered-down shit that Johnny serves."

The man smiled again. "I see you know him well."

"Fucking ought to."

The barman grabbed three beers and placed them on the stained drip mat. "I will be right back."

Kane took the twist top off his beer and took a pull. It was cold, but that was about it. He pulled a face. "Tastes like baboon piss."

Knocker shook his head. "No, that tastes sweeter."

Kagiso pulled a face and said, "You are right. I'm thinking hyena piss."

Kane pointed across the room. "Let's get a table."

They sat down and waited. A young waitress appeared. She wore a short skirt and a bikini top. "Can I get you gentlemen anything?"

Knocker shook his head. "No thanks, love. Me and my friend are working."

She looked at Kagiso. "What about you, sugar?"

"You couldn't handle me, *sugar*."

The waitress pulled a face and walked away. Kane looked at his friend. "Are you feeling okay?"

"A joint like this? Man would catch elephant pox or something to make his dick rot and fall off."

"Is that a thing?" Kane asked with a grin.

"It could be."

"I think your friend is coming, Raymond," Kagiso said, staring across the room.

"We really have to have a chat about you calling me Raymond, Kagiso," he said as he stared in the same direction as she was.

A tall man with dark hair and an expanding gut was coming toward them. He stopped in front of their table and said, "Ray Jensen. What the fuck brings you to a shit hole like this?"

Knocker held his beer up. "I was thirsty."

"Bullshit."

Knocker introduced the others.

"You didn't answer the question."

"How up to date are you on the poaching routes in the area?"

Johnny looked over to the bar and raised his hand. The person behind the bar nodded and grabbed a beer from the refrigerator before bringing it over. The former SAS man cracked it and took a pull before saying another word. "Talk like that could get a man in trouble around here, Ray."

"Are you saying you don't know, or not saying, Johnny?" Knocker asked.

The man rubbed at his stubbled chin. "Well, that depends. What is it you're looking for and what's it worth?"

"I thought we were friends, Johnny."

"We are, Ray, but a man has to make a living."

"I've got five hundred dollars in my pocket," Kane said to Johnny. "It's yours if you can tell us what we want to know."

Johnny gave Kane a thoughtful look. "All right, what do you want to know?"

"Hold it," Knocker said. "Don't fuck us around, Johnny."

"Who are you lot, anyway?" Johnny asked. "Why do you want to know?"

"Ever heard of Rassie Markram?"

"Who hasn't?" Johnny replied. "Why?"

"He's ventured into the world of poaching," Knocker told his friend.

"Why would he do that?"

"He's running out of money. He's got poaching crews in the field and he rolled over a deal in Vietnam.

Stole everything. His people killed some friends of ours."

Johnny seemed surprised. "Rassie Markram?"

"Yes."

"Poaching?"

"He's behind the coup in Cameroon as well," Kane informed him.

Johnny shook his head. "Yeah, can't help you."

Knocker's gaze grew hard. "What do you know, Johnny? And don't think I just bought that act just then. I know you better than that."

"I can't help you, Ray. Even if I knew he had buyers in Harare to shift ivory out of the country. Or an old airstrip outside the city, I wouldn't tell you."

Knocker looked puzzled. "What the fuck, Johnny?"

"Chinese, man, Christ. They own half the fucking country. They're the biggest buyers of ivory on the planet. If they find out I talked to you, I'm screwed. They probably know you're already here. By the time you passed under the Independence Memorial, they probably even knew your names."

"Is that who he has buying the ivory, Johnny?"

"For Christ's sake, Ray."

"Is that all?" Kane asked.

"Cowboy."

"What?"

He stared hard at Kane. "Cowboy. That's all I'm saying."

Kane placed the money on the table. "Thanks."

"Watch your backs. Especially two white guys with a Black girl. Some around still remember the old days."

They left the club and went to the van. They climbed in and Kane said, "Across the street in the blue Land Rover."

"Yeah, I saw them."

Knocker started the motor and pulled away from the sidewalk. As he drove away, Kane looked into the side mirror and saw three men climb out of the Land Rover.

"Go around the block."

Knocker turned right at the next intersection. Kagiso asked, "What are we doing?"

"Going back to the club to see who our friends back there are."

A couple of minutes later they pulled up outside the club again. Kane and Knocker screwed suppressors to their weapons and climbed out. Kane said to Kagiso, "Can you drive?"

"Yes."

"Then get ready."

They went inside and looked around. Not seeing Johnny anywhere, they walked over to the bar. "Where is he?" Knocker asked.

"In his office with—with those men."

"Who are they?"

"I don't know. I've never seen them before."

"Where is Johnny's office?" Knocker asked.

"Over there, through that door at the end of the hallway."

Kane looked around. "Get everyone out of here."

They walked over to the door and Kane eased it open. The hallway was empty. They were halfway along it when they heard the loud voices. Then came the sound of suppressed shots.

"Bollocks," Knocker said softly.

Moments later the door opened, and a man appeared. The suppressed P226 in Kane's hand came up and fired twice. The man dropped in the doorway, his body preventing the door from closing.

A hand appeared holding a weapon. Just as it fired, Kane and Knocker shouldered their way through doors on opposite sides of the hallway to get away from the firing line.

Bullets flew down the corridor and slammed into the door they had originally used. Holes appeared in it as the rounds punched through. Knocker leaned around the doorjamb and opened fire with his handgun.

Bullets smashed into the wall to the left of the doorway and the Brit took cover again as more bullets came his way. Kane fired and drew back. More bullets from the shooter in Johnny's office. Then the same shooter made the mistake of showing himself just enough for Knocker to get a calculated shot in which hit him in the face.

The shooter fell beside his dead friend.

Then silence.

There was meant to be three of them but no more shots came. Kane peered around the doorway and looked toward the office.

Nothing happened.

He fired a couple of shots hoping to draw the last shooter out, but no shots came. He looked across at his friend. "What do you think?"

"Go and have a look?"

"Why me?"

"You're our leader. Lead by example."

"Thanks."

Kane stepped out into the hallway while Knocker did his best to cover his advance. Pressed against the wall, Kane eased his way along until he reached the doorway. He peered around and nothing happened.

Knocker saw him disappear inside then moments later he reappeared and said, "It's clear."

The Brit joined Kane in the office and found Johnny seated in a chair with a hole in his head. "Shit."

"The last shooter went out the back door," Kane told him, pointing at the opening. "They're Asian. Most likely Chinese. Check their pockets. We'll see if it'll tell us anything."

Moments later when they had finished, Kane straightened and said, "Nothing. You?"

"Not a thing."

Kane nodded. "Take a picture and let's get out of here."

Using their phones, they took two pictures of the dead men. Knocker looked at his friend and shook his head. "What a bastard."

They left using the back door, the same as the surviving shooter. Then they went around the front and found the van gone.

Knocker said, "This girl has a habit of going off on her own."

————

WHEN THE LONE man came out of the alley and climbed into the Land Rover, Kagiso was torn about what to do. She watched him drive away and made her decision. She followed.

For twenty minutes he drove until pulling over at a laundromat. The man climbed out and went inside. Kagiso followed him. When she got inside she found that he had disappeared. Looking around, trying to see if he'd gone out the back, she caught the eye of the

Chinese woman at the counter who had finished with a customer and came over to her. "Can I help you?"

"My friend asked me to come and pick up a dress."

"Name?"

"Smith."

She gave her a suspicious look.

"First name?"

"Dawn."

"I'll have a look."

The Asian woman disappeared out the back. Kagiso looked around and saw the door off to the side. She hurried across to it and turned the handle. The door opened and she slipped through.

Kagiso was in a back room full of machinery and equipment. Women dressed in clothes a little more than rags worked the presses among clouds of white steam. None of them seemed to notice the stranger; they just worked as though in a trance.

She walked toward the rear of the room where a second door was. She tried it and found that one open too. On the other side was a hallway. At the end, a door. Voices echoed along it. Not that she could understand them.

"Hey, what are you doing?"

Kagiso tried not to jump at the sound of the voice. She turned and saw an Asian man staring hard at her. "I need to use the bathroom?"

"Not here. Go away."

Kagiso nodded. "Sorry."

"Go. Now."

She walked back to the door which led out into the service area. She could feel the man's eyes burning into her back.

She passed through and turned toward the counter.

The woman wasn't back. Kagiso shrugged and kept going out the door.

Once in the van, she heard her cell ringing on the seat where she'd left it. She picked it up. "Hello?"

"Where the hell are you?"

"I followed the car."

"You abandoned us is what you did. Now get back here."

He gave her directions. Then she started the motor and turned the vehicle around and drove away.

———

KANE WASN'T HAPPY. "Don't do that again."

"I followed the car," Kagiso repeated.

"Where to?"

"A laundry. A Chinese one."

"You shouldn't have left us."

"I'm sorry, it won't happen again."

"What did you find out?" Knocker asked her.

"Nothing."

"It has to be linked somehow. But it'll have to wait. I'll reach out to Slick and see what he can come up with."

"Where do you want to go now?" Kagiso asked.

"Back to our hotel. Until we get more intel, we're screwed."

———

KANE REACHED out to Swift and then waited for the tech to get back to him. Meanwhile, Knocker was watching the street below from their room. After a while, he said, "I think we have a watcher."

Kane walked over to where Knocker stood and looked. Kagiso joined them. The Brit pointed toward a dark Land Rover across the street in the middle of the mass of humanity which was Harare foot traffic. "It has been there a while. Two of them in it."

They watched them for a minute or two before Kane's cell buzzed. He answered. "Yes?"

It was Swift. "Okay, here is what I have. The two dead guys were Chinese nationals. They work for a branch of Chinese military that takes care of their interests overseas. You all know about the Belt and road initiative, well, it looks like they are into the buying and transportation of poached ivory. Big money in China, as you know. My guess is there is a corrupt official on the other end."

"What about the name Cowboy?"

"Wu Lei. According to his bio he loves western movies, which is where he gets his name from. He is a trafficker of sorts. Currently he's thought to be shipping ivory—get this—in boxes of dried abalone. The abalone is poached in South Africa and smuggled into Zimbabwe by road."

"Where do we find him?" Kane asked.

"He could be anywhere. He has a hangar at the airport, another at an airfield outside of Harare. Plus, a warehouse in the city, along with several other businesses."

"What about a laundry?"

"Hang on." Kane could hear him pounding the keys in the background. "He owns one of those too."

"All we have to do is find him."

"That's about it."

Kane nodded. "All right. Thanks."

The call disconnected and he turned to the others. "Airport, airfield, or warehouse?"

"Airport. Bribe customs officials and away you go," Knocker said.

"Fine, let's check it out."

———

BACK IN THEIR VEHICLE, they traversed the road to the Harare Airport. However, first they had to lose their tail, which, well versed in all standards of evasive driving, Knocker managed within three blocks.

As they drew closer to the airport Kagiso pointed out the side window. The two men looked and saw a giraffe seemingly gliding across the landscape with each side against the backdrop of grass and woodland. "It is called the Mukuvisi Woodlands," Kagiso told them. "If you look hard enough, you might even see a zebra."

Knocker said, "I knew it was there but never really thought much of it. Never even knew it had a name. Just trees and grass to me."

"You are a heathen, Raymond."

"So I've been told."

"Take this road here," Kane said. "It looks like it will take us around the back of where the freight hangars are situated."

Knocker turned off the asphalt road and onto a dirt one. The van rattled as it ran along the ungraded path, the corrugations almost shaking it to death. The Brit eased off the side trying to find smoother running.

"Stop here," said Kane and brought up his binoculars.

Knocker switched off the motor and looked toward the hangars. Kane swept left and right with the glasses, looking for anything that would indicate something untoward was happening.

At first there was nothing. Then he saw the first of the armed men. He was short, appeared to be Asian, and armed with a QCW-05 suppressed submachine gun. Kane watched him as he walked the front perimeter. Another appeared from a doorway. He too was armed.

The three sat and watched for the next hour, the sun baking down. "We can't stay here all day," Knocker said. "I vote we come back tonight and have a closer look."

Kane nodded and then stopped when he caught sight of a truck arriving. "Wait a minute."

He watched as it stopped outside the hangar. One of the guards walked around to the back, lifted the canvas tarpaulin which was draped across the load, and peered in.

The guard walked back around to the front and said something to the driver. Then the large door of the hangar slid open wide enough to swallow the truck.

"I vote I go and have a look," Kane said.

"I'm going with you," Knocker said, starting to move.

"No, wait here. I need someone to come and get me if something goes wrong." He reached for a case with the earwigs in it. He opened it and put one in, giving Knocker the other. "Come running if I holler."

"Roger that."

Kane climbed out of the van and started toward the hangars. Between him and his target, however, was a large chain-link fence. He followed it along for a few meters before finding a hole in it. Kane ducked down and slipped through.

On the other side of the fence, the brown grass was shorter. He paused momentarily and then jogged toward the hangar the truck had disappeared within. He peered around the corner looking for any guards, and found no one there.

Moving along the wall until he reached the corner, Kane looked around and found a smaller door.

Kane crept over and opened it, slipping inside. He hid behind a stack of pallets which were piled to the rear of the hangar. He looked around and the first think he saw was an old DC-3, a leftover relic from the bush war.

Then he saw the men standing around the truck. All were armed, one wore a cowboy hat. "I guess we found our man," Kane whispered.

"Cowboy?" asked Knocker over the earwig.

"Yes. Plus another six."

As Kane watched on, they gathered around the rear of the truck. They were talking about something and then the tarp was pulled back to reveal wooden crates. Long and narrow.

One of the armed guards grabbed the end of the crate and pulled it toward himself. Once the far end had reached the edge of the bed, another guard helped by grabbing that end.

They lifted it down and repeated the action until the truck was unloaded. Six crates.

One of the guards turned and started walking in his direction. Kane froze.

"Reaper, we have another two trucks headed your way," Knocker said over their comms.

Kane said nothing.

"Reaper?"

The man came closer. Kane reached for his handgun.

He heard the approaching trucks getting louder. A voice called out and the man stopped and turned. More words and he walked in the opposite direction.

Kane let out a long breath.

"Reaper?"

"I got you."

The large door opened once more and the next two trucks entered the hangar. When they pulled to a stop, spewing diesel fumes in the enclosed space, their drivers climbed out. This time the loads were emptied straight away. More boxes identical to the others.

"I need to get a look in these boxes," Kane said.

"Just ask," Knocker said.

Kane rolled his eyes but said nothing.

A couple of minutes later, the sound of a revving motor reached his ears. The Chinese men looked at each other in confusion. The sound of the motor grew louder and all of them went outside.

"I hope this works, Reaper," he heard Knocker say.

"So far so good," Kane said and came out from behind the pallets.

He hurried across to the crates, glanced at the door to make sure he was clear, and then opened one of them. Inside was a single elephant tusk.

Kane did a quick calculation in his head. With the price for ivory on the black market at an all-time high, multiply that per pound and then by the number of tusks he figured were there, Cowboy was now in possession of almost $7,000,000 in ivory.

Kane heard the van start again and took it as a signal to go. He hurried back to the pallets and made it just as Cowboy came back in followed by his men.

Kane then slipped out the rear door and hurried back to where the van was now waiting. He climbed in, and Knocker asked, "Well?"

"There was a lot of money came in on those trucks."

"What are we going to do?" Kagiso asked.

"First, we're going to burn that hangar. Then we're going to see a man about illegal ivory trafficking."

CHAPTER 12

MADIKWE GAME RESERVE, SOUTH AFRICA

The sun went down over the Madikwe Game Reserve with the sounds of hyenas laughing and a lion's roar. Strike Team Leopard and the squad of anti-poaching operators had been tracking the rhino for the past few days. To the east was another but they were using a tracking system to keep an eye on that one.

This one, affectionately known as Greg, was a large male with a cranky disposition. Blake had two people out. Troy Bosworth and one of the women from the anti-poaching squad. Their orders were to call in every hour. The last time they had been in radio contact was two hours before. Around ten p.m.

Blake crouched down beside his second in command, Mitch Potter. "They've missed two radio checks, Mitch. I think we need to go and have a look."

"How many?"

"You and me, Taja, and two others. Leave Robbie here."

"Righto."

Five minutes later they were walking out into the dark looking for their missing people.

They walked a perimeter and then expanded it. Still, they found nothing. Not even the rhino, Greg. Taja moved up beside Blake. "Something is wrong."

"I get that feeling too," Blake replied. "We should have found them by now, but not even the bloody rhino is around."

One of the anti-poaching girls approached them. "We have found the rhino."

"Where?"

"Come see."

They followed her for a hundred meters before she stopped. Taja spoke to her and then she turned to Blake. "Your flashlight."

"What about it?"

"Turn it on."

The team leader grabbed his flashlight and turned it on.

Immediately the beam hit the leathery gray object in front of them. The rhino lay on its side, unmoving. Blake walked around the front of it and saw that its horn was missing. "Fucking bollocks. Why the hell didn't we hear it?"

Taja bent down and picked something up. She held it out for Blake to see. "This should explain."

"A tranquilizer dart. They hit it with that then cut the poor bastard's throat before taking the horn. Shit."

"Doesn't explain where Troy went."

Blake looked around. He instantly turned the flashlight off and stood in silence. Then, "Did you hear it?"

"Nothing," replied Mitch.

"It was a gunshot," Taja said.

Blake nodded. "I thought so."

As they stood in the darkness and listened, in the distance the sound of more shots reached out across the grassland. "Someone is attacking the camp," Blake hissed as he unslung his assault rifle. "Move."

———

BY THE TIME they reached the camp it was all over. The shooting had ceased, and the shooters were gone, leaving behind the bodies of the dead. Not one person was left alive. Those who had only been wounded, had been executed with a bullet to the head.

Robbie, the man they had left behind, was one of those. Blake looked down at his body and felt his anger rise. "Bastards."

"What are we going to do?" Mitch asked the Team Leopard leader.

"I want to go after the pricks but if we leave the bodies like this, the scavengers will tear them apart. Then there are the two we still have missing."

"Not anymore," Taja said as she came out of the darkness. She pointed over her shoulder. "I found them fifty meters that way. Their throats were cut."

"Damn it. Mitch, reach out to Bravo. Tell them what is happening. Taja, come with me. We're going for a walk."

"Whoa, boss, what are you up to?"

"Scouting. Don't worry, it's recon only. Just secure this area and get a chopper in here."

"You don't even know which way they went," Mitch pointed out.

"They went east," Taja said.

"We'll be fine. Just get the chopper."

"Will do."

Blake and Taja walked off into the darkness.

———

By MORNING they had found the hole in the fence used by the poachers to gain access to the park. The sun was coming up over the reserve bathing it in orange. Already the animals were calling to each other, the zebras particularly vocal.

Somewhere in the early morning before daylight they had picked up some brown hyenas which had insisted on following them.

Using the zippy ties which were meant for poachers —if they caught any—Blake and Taja pulled the fence together and blocked the hole as best they could.

Then they continued.

As soon as it was light enough, Taja examined the tracks more closely. "Ten men. White men."

"How do you know?" Blake asked.

"Their boots and the way they walk."

The team leader nodded. "All right. How far ahead of us?"

"A couple of hours." She nodded toward a high ridge dotted with rocks and brush. "There will be someone up there watching."

"Why do you say that?"

"Because it is what they do," replied Taja.

"Which way did they go?" Blake asked.

"To the east still."

"Then act like you've lost the trail. We'll circle around the ridge and see if we can come up on whoever is up there."

For the next hour, Taja led Blake around the ridge,

stopping frequently as though the trail had vanished. Then once they were out of sight of the front side, they started climbing.

It was almost noon when they topped the ridge and began making their way along, not sky-lining them-selves in case they were spotted. Twenty minutes after crossing the crest, Taja stopped and sat on her haunches. "Down there near the orange rock."

At first Blake saw nothing, then he picked out the faint wisp of tobacco smoke giving away the poacher's position. If this had been one of his men, he would have torn shreds off them and then kicked them off the team.

"Dumb," he muttered.

"Yes," Taja agreed.

Blake brought up his 417 and started walking toward the rock. He went slowly, carefully picking where he placed his foot each time, so as not to move a stone or stand on a stick.

At last they reached the rock and Blake moved around it. There, sitting with his shoulder against the rough surface, his weapon leaning beside him, was a white man dressed in bush camouflage clothing.

"If you move, I will kill you," Blake said, his voice low, menacing.

The poacher froze.

"Taja, get his weapon."

Taja stepped in swiftly and took the gun. Blake moved around to the front of the man so he could see his face. Then he hit him with the 417's butt, opening a cut in the man's cheek, releasing a flow of blood.

The poacher grunted and straightened up. Blake's eyes narrowed. "Kill my people, you fucking prick."

"I don't know what you're talking about." The man was South African.

"No? We followed you and your people all the way here. I was going to kill you—kill all of you. But I'm not going to. I've got something else in store for you."

———

THE SHORT-WHEELBASE LAND Rover Series III bounced over a large wallow and dodged the rhino as it tried to ram the swerving vehicle. Tied to the front, the poacher howled in protest at the prospect of dying such a brutal death.

Blake floored the gas pedal and the Land Rover shot forward once again, putting distance between the vehicle and the rhino.

When he figured there to be enough gap, the Leopard team leader turned off the ignition and climbed down. He walked around the front and stared at the battered form which had been whipped by thick stalked grass and brush. "Had enough?"

The man nodded.

"What's your name?"

"Thomas."

"Where do you come from?"

"Rassie—Rassie Markram."

"Where is your camp?"

"The river. East."

"How many?"

"Forty," Thomas said.

"Why so many?"

"More poaching teams."

"Why kill all my people?"

"We saw your camp. Got your man and the Black whore before we got the rhino."

Blake felt his anger rise. "Why kill the rest?"

"Why not? Most are only Black whores."

"That's the second time you said that; don't make it a third," Blake warned him.

The man was becoming braver.

"Fucking whores we killed got what they deserved."

Blake shrugged. "Okay."

He untied the poacher and pulled him free from the front of the Land Rover. "I warned you."

The Leopard team leader shot him in the leg. The man cried out and fell to the ground. "I'm giving you a chance. It's more than the others got."

"What?"

"I just hope you can move faster than the rhino."

He stared up at Blake. "What?"

"Then there are the lions and hyenas. Either way, you're fucked."

"You can't leave me here," the poacher pleaded.

"Yeah, I can."

Suddenly the rhino appeared out of the scrub. Blake looked at the poacher and saw the fear on his face. "I guess we're about to find out if you can run or not. I hope the creature gives you as good as you gave the one last night."

"Don't leave me," the poached blurted as he struggled to his feet.

Ignoring him, Blake and Taja climbed back into the Land Rover. The motor ticked over, and the gears grated as the stick moved. Then the vehicle started driving away. The poacher shouted after them, telling them to stop. And as his pleas fell on deaf ears, over 3,000 pounds of beast bore down on him.

———

Blake shook hands with Roberts of Mamba and said, "Thanks for coming out, Roy."

"The least I could do," the Mamba leader replied. "What do you know?"

"They're over on the river to the east. Got a camp there. Rassie Markram's men."

"How many?" Roberts asked.

"Forty, so I believe."

"Then we'd better shut them down."

CHAPTER 13

HARARE, ZIMBABWE

While Leopard were deep in trouble, Kane, Knocker, and Kagiso went back to the hangar at the airport. They parked outside the fence and entered via the hole which Kane had used that afternoon.

This time, however, they were dressed for combat, wearing body armor, webbing, and carrying their M6s. They crossed through the grass toward the hangar, moving in a short column. When they reached it, there was a light on inside.

Knocker and Kagiso followed Kane around to the rear and they entered through the door which was still unlocked.

Kane eased the door open wide enough for the Brit to pass through. Once inside, he took up position behind the same pallets Kane had used earlier.

He immediately saw two men sitting on chairs. Both were armed. They looked to have Chinese military weapons. Using hand signals, Knocker conveyed what he was seeing to the others and Kane nodded. Then, more hand signals and they brought their suppressed M6A2s up and stepped out into the open, walking forward.

Both of them fired twice. The two armed men pitched forward off their seats onto the concrete floor. The Team Reaper pair searched for more threats, and when they were certain there were none, they lowered their weapons.

Kane said, "Looks like more trucks turned up after we left. There are more crates than there was before."

"Let's have a look," Knocker said.

He opened a crate and found a tusk. In the next he found something completely different. "They've been killing hippos."

"Bastards."

"They are animals," Kagiso said, walking up behind them.

Knocker glanced at her. "I would have used harsher words, but that will do."

"Fuck," she hissed.

The Brit shook his head. "Now don't start that."

"Let's get these charges planted and get out of here," Kane said. "Check the fuel on the plane. It might come in handy when the charges blow. Kagiso, keep watch."

Five minutes later, the explosive devices were set to go. Knocker had found fuel in the DC-3 and placed a charge over the fuel cell.

"Everything is set, Reaper," the Brit informed his friend. "Five minutes and up she goes."

"All right, let's get out of here."

They left the same way they'd entered. Out through the back under what was now a clear sky instead of the partial cloud they had on the way in. By the time they reached the van, there was only about a minute left to go.

While they were taking off their combat gear, the charges blew, sending a large fireball into the sky. Kane placed his weapon in the van and said, "We'd better get out of here before airport security arrives."

They climbed in and disappeared into the dark, the hangar, and millions of dollars in ivory well alight.

———

BACK AT THE HOTEL, Kane reached out to Ferrero. All their weapons, apart from their handguns, and their gear was in a special compartment in the floor of the van. Kane told Ferrero about the night raid and that everything had gone well. But he sensed that something was not right on the other end.

Ferrero told him about Leopard.

"Damn it," Kane growled. "What's happening?"

"Cara dispatched a helicopter to bring in the bodies. She also sent Mamba out to see if they could locate the camp and shut it down."

"Who said come to Africa?" Kane muttered.

"What is your next part of the plan?" Ferrero asked.

"We'll go after Cowboy," Kane informed him.

"Do you want more support?"

"We'll just need a way out of Harare when we get him, and maybe Slick on ISR," Kane replied.

"By when?"

"Tomorrow night. I'll let you know when we have his pos nailed down. Can you get Slick to hook me up in the morning?"

"Will do. Take care, Reaper. And don't start a war

with the Chinese. That's the last thing we want. Intel has a quick response team in country looking after assets. You don't want them coming down on you."

"I'll try to be good."

———

SWIFT AND KANE talked just after nine the following morning. The tech had been putting together a brief about their target. "He's former Chinese military. Did you know that?"

"I do now," Kane replied.

"The wires have been busy this morning as well. I hooked into their communications network and gleaned a few things. The ivory you burned was bound for Shanghai. The recipient was a former Chinese politician. He'd bought the ivory from Markram and paid for it. Since Cowboy works for Markram, the buyer is holding him responsible. Now he wants his money back, but Markram isn't budging."

Swift continued. "The Chinese have special investigators in the country who take care of interests and they're working the case. So you'll need to watch your back."

"Where can I find Cowboy?" Kane asked.

"He has a suite in a building in the center of Harare. I'll send you the address. It's a high rise and it is on the top floor with a pool on the rooftop. Your mission, Jim, should you choose to accept it, is—"

"Slick, just spit it out."

"You'll need to get up there through his security, take him, and get to the extract point."

"We can do that."

"Quietly?"

Kane looked at Knocker and raised an eyebrow. "Maybe not."

"If you don't want to bring all of Harare down on top of you, you'll get it done."

"Are we sure that kidnapping Cowboy will affect Markram?" Kane asked the tech.

"It'll affect him, all right. Cowboy is his middleman in Zimbabwe. Everything he poaches in that area goes through the little prick. You take him out, you fuck up one of Markram's routes. Take out enough of his routes and you'll have one very pissed off diamond miner. Then you'll be able to get him."

"Where is the extract?"

"Two blocks south of the building."

"Fuck me," Knocker muttered. "It might as well be a hundred fucking miles."

Kane shook his head. "It's no good, Slick. We need extract closer. Give me a look at the building. The top."

A picture flashed up and Kane saw the pool covering most of the space available. He said, "The chopper can take us off the rooftop."

"I don't know, Reaper, it's a bit tight."

"He won't have to touch down, just pick us up."

"Fine. When?"

"Tonight."

———

"How many floors?" Kane asked Knocker.

"I got fifteen," the Brit replied. "Long way up."

"Better than risking the elevator."

Knocker nodded. "Without a doubt."

Kagiso looked at them in disbelief. "You two are

very crazy if you even contemplate climbing up the outside."

"We'll go from balcony to balcony," Kane told her. "It'll be a cinch."

Agreeing with the assessment, Knocker said, "Once we reach the suite, we'll enter, take Cowboy to the rooftop, and catch our ride home."

"I cannot believe I am going to do this."

"Get into your kit. Leave nothing behind."

Five minutes later they were scaling the outside of the building in the dark like they were some kind of Marvel superheroes.

It was simple enough. Reach a balcony, climb onto the balustrade, reach for the one above, and haul themselves up. Then repeat many times.

"I'm so glad we don't have forty floors to do," Knocker growled in a low voice over his comms.

On floor eleven, things became interesting for a few minutes. Kane and Kagiso had climbed past but just as Knocker grabbed the base of the balustrade to pull himself up, the couple in the room it belonged to came out through the sliding door. Both stood at the rail and looked out at the night. Knocker knew if they looked down, he was screwed. But for some reason, they didn't, and after a couple of minutes, turned and went back inside.

The former SAS man pulled himself up and then hurriedly did the same up to twelve.

They paused on fourteen. The apartment was dark, indicating that whoever was there was asleep, or it was vacant. Once they were set, Knocker said, "I'll go first."

He climbed up and over the rail, and dropped to the tiled balcony, crouching low, waiting for Kagiso and Kane to join him.

Once they were up, he approached the sliding door and tried it. The door was open. That was the problem with people these days. When they were so high up, they thought they were secure. Obviously, they never heard of the spiderman thief. Or special forces.

Knocker took out his suppressed P226 and entered the suite illuminated by digital clocks and small standby lights, Kane and Kagiso behind him. Someone was asleep on the sofa. The Brit walked over to him and placed the weapon against Sleeper's forehead. "Wake up, motherfucker."

Eyes snapped open. Knocker's hand clamped across the man's mouth. "Make a sound and I'll fuck you up."

The man just stared at the armed intruder leaning over him. "Now, how many?"

Words were muffled behind the hand.

The Brit said, "Just blink. Besides you, how many?"

He blinked twice.

"Where?"

The man's eyes slid one way and then the other. The first direction was the bedroom. That had to be Cowboy. The second direction was the...bathroom.

The door opened and a man walked out. He was armed. Who takes a weapon to the bathroom in the middle of the night?

Knocker shot him. Twice.

WHAP! WHAP!

The man dropped where he stood. No time to comprehend what was happening.

"Fuck," Knocker hissed softly, admonishing himself. He looked at the man who'd been sleeping. "Do not bloody move."

He looked over at Kane who was already moving toward the bedroom door, his own weapon up and aimed at the door. He burst through but it was too late. The smuggler known as Cowboy already had his cell in his hand.

"Drop it," Kane snarled. "Do it or I'll put a bullet in you."

"Who are you?" Cowboy demanded. "What do you want?"

Kane noticed he still had the cell. He strode forward and grabbed it. It was transmitting to someone. Kane threw it on the floor hard enough for it to come apart. He forced Cowboy onto his face on the bed and zip-tied his hands.

Dragging him to his feet he shoved him roughly toward the open bedroom door. As they moved into the main room of the suite, Kane forced the smuggler down onto his knees. He looked at Knocker and said, "Get that chopper in here, the bastard has sounded the alarm."

Knocker started transmitting to the helicopter while Kane turned to Kagiso. "Watch the hallway. Someone is coming."

Kagiso unlimbered her M6A2 and hurried across to the door. She cracked it a little and was able to peer along the hallway. It took only a couple of minutes for two men to appear carrying QCW-05s, while the others were getting their prisoners ready to travel.

The new team member brought up the suppressed M6A2 and fired at the first target.

Two 5.56 rounds punched into his chest, and he fell to the red carpeted floor. The second man responded quickly enough to bring his weapon up and open fire. Bullets punched into the wall around the room doorway forcing Kagiso back.

"It is time to go," she called over to the others before returning fire at the shooter in the hallway.

Kane and Knocker dragged the two prisoners to their feet and shoved them forward. Kagiso was still firing when suddenly she forced her way out into the hallway, advancing on her target.

The shooter took three rounds in the chest, and he fell to the floor not far from his companion.

Kane called out to Kagiso. "Get to the stairwell. Go up and secure the rooftop."

She disappeared and Kane and Knocker followed as quickly as they could move their charges. When they reached the stairwell, they forced their prisoners up the stairs.

"You do not know who you are messing with," Cowboy protested.

"How about you tell me, dickhead," the Brit growled.

"Rassie Markram. That's who. The man will find you and gut you like a fish."

Knocker shoved him away. "I hope so, Davy Crockett. I want to cut the bastard's heart out."

The rooftop was clear. Kane called the helicopter in, and the machine appeared off to the west. It came in low before coming to a hover just above the rooftop. Kane and Knocker forced Cowboy and his bodyguard on and the three of them climbed aboard. Then within moments, the helicopter pulled up and away. Mission complete.

———

SOUTH AFRICA

Roberts crouched down with Ted Clarke and Blake and said, "It's all quiet. Looks like they are sleeping."

"Guards?"

"Nothing to worry about."

"What are our orders?" Clarke asked.

"Ever heard the saying, kill them all and let God sort them out?"

"Uh-huh."

"There's your answer. We'll show Markram the error of his ways. They showed our people no mercy, they get the same in return."

"Roger that."

Roberts said to Blake, "You want to do the honors?"

Blake nodded. "Everyone standby. Terror One this is Leopard One, over."

"Copy, Leopard One."

"Cleared hot, I say again, cleared hot. Send them to hell."

"Roger, Leopard One. Terror One inbound."

Less than two minutes later, a MH-6 Little Bird came in low across the African landscape, twin rotary cannons flaming hell upon the poachers' camp.

Within a heartbeat, it had pulled up, turned on an invisible dime, and started another gun run.

The tearing sound ripped across the darkened sky and the impacts of the gunfire could be heard through the night. After one more run, the pilot radioed in. "Leopard One, we're pulling out and taking up sniper cover, over."

"Copy. Ground element moving in."

The team made their way into what was left of the camp and started mopping up the poachers. By the time it was over, nothing was left. They had exacted revenge for their people and sent Rassie Markram a message. He'd declared war but they were going to win it.

———

YAOUNDÉ, CAMEROON

The news Galloway brought to his boss just added insult to injury. He had flown in from Douala to Yaoundé that day. The team in South Africa was gone. Added to what happened in Zimbabwe, he was losing even more money, which was not supposed to be happening.

Markram glared at Galloway. "Tell the team in Kenya to tighten security."

"The ivory we have there is almost ready to ship."

"Well, I don't want anything to go wrong with it. What about Cowboy?"

"As far as we know, they still have him."

"I don't like it. Have Kenya speed up their end. I want that ivory on a ship out of Mombasa as soon as possible."

The door to the office opened. Markram had set up in an office in the National Assembly Building after Omossola had taken over. Markram looked at the doorway and saw Chernov. "What can I do for you, Nikita?"

"A little bird told me that your bad luck is growing."

"A minor setback."

"When do I get my diamonds?"

"Just as soon as the mine is operational. It isn't that far away."

Chernov shook his head. "I do not understand,

Rassie. We took the mines virtually intact. They just needed workers. Why the hold up?"

"Patience, Nikita. In the meantime, I have another mission for you."

"Why can't your people do it?" Chernov asked.

"Because they are currently engaged mopping up pockets of resistance."

"Your missions seem to cost me men," Chernov pointed out.

"If this works, we won't have to worry about those mercenaries anymore."

"Fine, tell me."

CHAPTER 14

MOSEKI CAMP, TWO DAYS LATER

All teams, apart from a small group from the anti-poaching squad, were back at base licking their wounds. The people from Global had been running and gunning for too many days and they needed a break.

So, it was beer and sleep. Kane was in the camp's rec room playing chess against Kagiso. It was his way of gauging her. Knocker was reading a book Cara had given him about the SAS in World War Two. Brick was reading a Ludlum novel and Lofty was doing a jigsaw puzzle that he'd found neglected on a table in the corner.

"Piece of shit," he muttered.

"What's up?" Rani asked, looking up from her crossword.

"All the pieces aren't here."

She nodded. "Yeah, I hate it when that happens."

Teller was sitting at a separate table with a pencil in hand sketching in a scrapbook. "You know, there are places that will take pictures you send them and put them on puzzles."

As Kayla walked past, she stared down at the picture. It was an elephant. She nodded, surprised at the skill he was showing. "That is like the beast. Magnificent."

"Thank you."

"Where did you learn to do that?" she asked.

"I just always had it."

"It is a great talent."

"Can you sketch?" he asked her.

Kayla smiled at him. "As far as drawing goes, I make a great brain surgeon."

Teller grinned at her.

She walked over and sat next to Knocker. "Hello, Raymond."

He glanced at her. "Don't call me that."

"Why not, it's your name."

"People tend to call me Raymond when I've done something wrong," he explained.

"I think it is a good name. A strong name."

He placed the book in his lap. "All right, what is it?"

"My girls need some extra hand-to-hand combat training."

"Fine."

Kayla looked surprised, as though she had expected him to say no. "Tomorrow?"

He nodded. "If something doesn't come up."

"Checkmate," Kagiso said, and her broad smile revealed white teeth.

Kane shook his head and Knocker said, "Brick, you owe me twenty."

"Damn it, Reaper, how did you lose?" Brick growled.

Kane turned his head to stare at his friend. "You bet against me? Some friend you are."

"You're just a shit chess player. Besides, I've seen Kagiso in action."

"Thanks, buddy."

"I'm not complaining. I won twenty bucks."

"I'm bored," Rani said aloud.

"Christ," Knocker growled.

Lofty stared at her. "That was a stupid thing to say."

"What? Why?"

"Because you start saying things like that, and shit always happens."

"That's right," Knocker agreed. "Go and find one of the other team guys. Have a roll in the sack, just don't say—"

Cara appeared. "Heads up. We have a mission."

"You're bloody bored."

"Shit," Kane growled and glared at Rani. "You had to say it."

Lofty gave her a disappointed look. "Thank you."

"Aw, come on, guys."

As Brick walked past her, he placed an arm around her shoulders and said, "You owe us beer."

———

"Our friend Cowboy gave us some intel which we've been running down," Cara explained. "The results led us to Kenya."

"Home of a few of the more lovely terror groups known to man," Knocker replied in a droll tone.

"Yes, but Markram has been using one of the local gangs to run that end of his operation. A lot like

Cowboy, they take possession, then move it on through ships headed for China."

"What is the plan?" Kane asked.

"Two-fold. Markram has a shipment due to leave Friday night. Two nights from now. First, you're going to set charges and sink the ship."

"Where?"

"Set the charges to go off once the ship has left harbor."

"That's assuming that it leaves on time."

"Yes."

"You said two-fold," Kane reminded Cara.

"Yes, the second part of the mission is this man."

A picture appeared on the large screen. The man was Asian. Presumably Chinese. "Zhang Han. One of the major buyers of illegal ivory and rhino horn in China. Very rarely comes out of his home country, and when he does, he's usually back safe in bed by the time authorities know he's been. However, he is in Mombasa. We don't know why, but we do know where. It is a small window, but the head shed believes you can get him."

"Two teams," Kane said.

Knocker nodded. "I agree."

"All right, what do you suggest?"

Kane said, "We'll take Han, Mamba place the charges on the ship."

Roberts nodded. "We can do that."

Cara nodded. "All right. We can support both. We'll have a RHIB on standby for Mamba just in case, and a helo for Reaper."

"Where is this guy, anyway?" Brick asked.

Cara grinned. It was almost wicked. "You are going to love this. There is a hotel in Mombasa—"

"We were just in a hotel. It's getting kind of cliché. You'd think someone would tell the bad guys to stay somewhere different."

"Are you done?"

"Yes, ma'am."

"As I was saying, there is a hotel in Mombasa where he usually stays. This time, however, he's staying at a mansion outside of Mombasa, a gated Chinese community with Chinese security."

"Must have heard we were coming," Lofty said.

"Watch your backs. The security they use are former Chinese Special Forces. Sea Dragon Commandos. Not only westerners are targets for the terror groups in Kenya."

"So, we secure Han, then get the hell out of there on a chopper," Kane said.

Cara nodded. "That's the plan."

"Why can't we go after Markram instead of dicking around?" Knocker asked.

"Because he's still locked away in Cameroon. Hopefully, if we cause him enough pain, he'll stick his head across the border, and we can chop it off."

"I wish he'd do it sooner rather than later. This operation seems to be dragging."

"Eyes on the prize, Raymond. We're still doing good," Cara said.

Knocker mumbled something unintelligible and then went quiet. Kane put up his hand.

Cara nodded at him. "Yes?"

"Any word from Cameroon?"

"Nothing much. They're getting the diamond mines operational, and rebel forces are mopping up pockets of resistance with Markram's men helping."

"Any word on putting troops back in?"

Cara hesitated. "You didn't hear this from me, but I've been told there are several SAS teams working in country getting foreigners out."

She waited for any other questions. When there was nothing, she nodded and said, "All right. Get your teams ready and form a plan. We'll get you all the intel we can to make your mission easier."

The briefing broke up and straight away Kane started getting his people organized.

"Knocker, teach Kagiso what to do for getting ready to deploy on a big op. Brick, see the doc about medical supplies. Lofty, you're with me. We need to get all the intel together. We all meet up in an hour to go over it. Roger?"

They all nodded and went their separate ways.

———

"Do we want the M6s?" Kagiso asked Knocker.

The Brit shook his head. "No, grab the MP5SDs. If it kicks off, it'll probably be CQB. Although, grab a 417 with laser and night sights on it. We might need to set up an overwatch."

Kagiso grabbed weapons and ammunition. "Same handguns?"

"Yes. Also grab the new Nods. The white phosphorus ones."

She saw him grab grenades. "You think we will need them?"

"Never can be too careful."

"How will we approach the target?" she asked.

"Probably parachute. Have you ever done it?"

Kagiso nodded. "Once."

"Well, you must have done it right, you're still alive. Over there in that box, you'll find ELO."

Kagiso stared at him. "The band? Is it a CD?"

Knocker laughed. "Experimental ammunition. Electronically Loaded Ordnance. The boffins at Global have been working on it. We've never used them before."

"What do they do?"

"They're fired from a handgun. Somehow when they hit their target, they release an electronic charge which incapacitates them. Harmless unless you have a heart condition. Pack two mags each. If we need more than that we have our MP5s."

They finished putting things together and went to meet up with the others. Kane and Lofty were already waiting. Brick joined them moments after. The team gathered around a table that held a map of the immediate area of the gated community, and folders of intel.

"How are we getting in?" Kane asked.

"We have two choices," said Lofty. "Parachute, or by road."

"Parachute," Knocker said. "There is a LZ right there about five hundred meters from the fence."

"Why not road?" Kane asked.

"More chance of us getting picked up," Brick said. "Parachute gives us the benefit of stealth."

"All right, we jump. Weapons?"

"MP5SDs," Knocker informed him. "CQB. Also, we loaded the ELO ammo. No time like the present."

"Fine. We'll need a cutting tool to get through the fence. It'll more than likely have razor wire on top. Could be electrified as well."

"I'll make sure we have something. We packed the new NODs as well. They seem to be good."

Kane placed a finger on the map. "Han is here. We need to get from here to here without tipping our hand."

"There will be security," Kagiso said. "They will also have dogs."

"We can fix that," Brick said. "A little concoction I like to call No Dogs."

"Ah, fuck, not that stuff," Knocker growled.

"It works," the former SEAL reminded him.

"Yeah, because it smells like two-day-old roadkill out in the desert."

Kagiso chuckled. "It cannot be that bad."

"Don't you believe it."

"Okay, we get this far," Kane said, pointing at the mansion with his finger. "What next?"

"Secure the guards and then the target," Lofty said. "We do it quietly. If we get sprung, we go hard for the HVT and worry about the rest later."

Kane looked at the others. "Agreed?"

They all nodded.

"Right, now for extract. We can't get a helicopter in there. Which means we must go to it."

"They've got vehicles," Knocker said. "We take one of them."

"Okay. Let's get back to the ELO ammo. It's untried in combat."

Knocker nodded. "Yes, but the last thing I want to do is leave a bunch of dead Chinese operators in our wake. They're there to protect the whole community, not one man. When it comes to Han's bodyguards, we can put them down if need be."

"All right, but if it turns out to be a threat to the team, then we go live."

"I have no issue with that."

Kane nodded. "Now we need a plan B."

Knocker grinned. "Shoot everything and run like hell."

"Good plan. Any questions?"

There were none.

"Okay. Let's sort out details."

———

KILINDINI HARBOR, MOMBASA

Roberts came up the hawser on the bow of the *Shanghai Express* and waited for the rest of his men. Once they were on board the ship the Mamba team leader brought his MP5SD up and started to move through the deck containers toward the hatch which would lead them into the bowels of the ship.

The four of them remained silent as they crept through narrow openings. Back at base, elements of Bravo were watching their every move.

"Mamba, hold." The voice sounded urgent. "You have a tango coming up on your three."

Just because Roberts couldn't see them, didn't mean the sentry wasn't there. The roamer was obviously coming toward him through an opening such as the one he and the team were traversing.

He let his MP5 drop on its strap and took out his combat knife. He waited. In his ear, he heard Teller say, "Three...two...one...now."

The sentry appeared on beat and Roberts readied himself like a coiled spring. But, instead, the sentry turned away and kept walking.

Roberts let out a long breath and waited for the man to disappear.

Ted Clarke took over point and they continued creeping toward the hatch. Their aim was to get down to the engine room, hide the explosives, and get off safely.

Reaching the end of the shipping container row, they paused. Teller said, "You are clear to the hatch. Once you are below deck, you're on your own. I can't see a thing."

Clarke edged forward and then crossed the gap to the hatch. Moments later, Mamba disappeared off the screen.

———

"ALL REAPER CALLSIGNS down and in play," Kane said over the comms. "Moving to target."

"Copy, Reaper One, you're moving to the target."

With Brick on point, they made their way toward the perimeter of the gated community. Once they arrived, Knocker took out a small cutting torch and opened the chain-mesh fence enough for them to pass through.

While he did that, Kane said over his comms, "Bravo One, put the cameras on a loop."

"One step ahead of you."

On the other side, they drew their P226s and loaded them with ELO magazines. From there it was a matter of using the shadows to approach their target building.

Knocker took point and guided them through the streets, avoiding streetlamps and patrols with the help of Rani. Then they reached the perimeter of the target.

A fence surrounded it. They crouched down in the

shadows before getting the all-clear to commence their infiltration.

Using the cutting torch again, Knocker made a hole in this fence as well. Done, he stowed the torch in his webbing, and they entered and started toward the main house.

"Hold, hold, hold," Rani said urgently. "Danger close."

They all dropped to their faces on the damp grass and waited. A sentry appeared. He was armed and walking in their general direction. Knocker gripped his weapon tighter, hoping that the sentry would veer away.

But he didn't.

Shit.

The P226 in Knocker's hand with the ELO rounds came up and he fired once. They were low velocity and through the suppressor, they made virtually no noise. The round hit the sentry in the chest and the electric charge it housed shot through the man's body, knocking him out.

"Well, that works," the Brit said in a low voice. He secured the unconscious sentry and gagged him. Then hid him in the shadows.

They moved on to the main house, circling around to a side door which opened out onto a sandstone paved area with a pergola.

"Bravo, you have two guards coming around the corner of the house in three..."

Kane dropped out the ELO mag.

"Two..."

He reloaded with live rounds.

"One..."

The P226 came up and aimed.

"Now."

On cue, the two guards appeared.

Kane shot one in the face with his first and the second one died with two in his chest as he scrambled to comprehend what had just happened.

Then Reaper turned to Knocker. "Get us in that fucking house, now."

———

THE SHIP'S interior smelled like salt and diesel oil. Mamba made their way down into the bowels of the freighter as stealthily as they could. Twice they'd had to dodge one of the crew but there were no guards below deck. Now they were entering the hatch into the engine room.

"Get the charges placed," Roberts ordered his people.

Five minutes and the job was completed. The timers were set to go off after the ship had left the harbor.

"All done?" the Mamba boss asked Clarke.

"Ready to go, Roy."

Now all they had to do was get back topside and to the rendezvous with the RHIB.

So far, so good.

———

IN THE KITCHEN, Knocker shot a bodyguard, blood now pooling around the corpse. He and Brick cleared the ground floor. A second bodyguard was in the living room watching late night television. Brick came up behind him and shot him in the back of the head.

Kane, Lofty, and Kagiso went upstairs. Intel had Han in a room toward the rear of the house. When they found him, they woke him by placing the barrel of a SIG against his forehead.

"Good evening," Kane said to Han. "Sorry about the rude awakening but you need to come with us."

"Who are you?" Han managed to ask.

"Get up."

Han climbed out of bed and Kane secured him. Just as he was about to gag him and put a bag over his head, Han tipped the bedside stand over so that it crashed to the floor.

Kane muttered a curse. "Try that again, asshole, and I'll bury—"

The door to one of the upstairs bedrooms opened and a man appeared with a weapon. Lofty turned and brought up his MP5 and hit him with a short burst. The man collapsed to the floor but on his way down, he squeezed the trigger of the compact submachine gun and sprayed the floor with a loud burst.

"Bloody hell," Lofty growled. "That's fucking torn it."

"Kagiso, cover the hallway. Lofty, let's get him ready to travel."

Kagiso dropped to a knee and waited. It took only moments before another door opened and an armed guard appeared. She fired before he even knew what was happening, making him fall beside his comrade.

Gunfire sounded from the floor below. Kane said into his comms, "Reaper Two, sitrep?"

"You lot woke the bloody house up. Now we're going to have to fight our way out of here."

"Reaper One, from Bravo One, I'm starting to see a lot of activity coming your way."

"Roger that. We have our package, and we need to extract."

"It might be a little warm down there."

"Rooftop, Reaper," Lofty said. "It's flat and the helicopter won't have to touch down."

"Did you get that, Rani?"

"Copy."

"Make it happen." He paused then said, "All call-signs, we're going up."

———

ROBERTS PAUSED and waited for the sailor to walk past their hidden position. When he was gone, they stepped out onto the walkway once more and kept moving through the ship.

A deep rumbling started down in the bowels of the ship and Roberts paused. He turned to Clarke. "The ship is getting ready to sail."

"They're early. What now?"

"Keep moving."

Reaching the top deck five minutes later, they became concerned that the ship was moving. They crouched in the shadows beside a container. "Bravo, we have a problem."

"I see that, Mamba One. We're redeploying the RHIB. Once you're out of the harbor, go over the side and it'll pick you up."

"Roger that."

Clarke said, "Looks like the charges will go off when the ship is at sea."

"They've got lifeboats. They'll be fine."

The small group remained where they were for the next thirty minutes before the call came in. "Mamba, this is Bravo. RHIB is in position. You're clear of the harbor. Time to go."

"Roger. Let them know we're coming overboard."

Roberts looked at his men. "Good luck. When you hit, go deep to stay away from the propellers. And swim away."

After they had gone over the side, no one was any the wiser that they had been on the ship.

―――――

Knocker took up position where he could watch their six while the others set a perimeter on the rooftop, waiting for the incoming helicopter.

They could hear voices coming from below as Han's guards came running. Several tried the stairwell but were met with a withering fusillade of fire.

Lights flashed from across the estate as the call for assistance went out and the security started to converge on the mansion.

"Here comes the cavalry," Brick said. "What do you want us to do, Reaper?"

"Keep their heads down."

The approaching vehicles came to a sliding halt as they were fired upon. Their occupants jumped out and scattered. Suddenly the night came alive as a Black Hawk swooped in low over the mansion.

"Reaper One, this is Dark Horse One-One, copy?"

"Read you Lima Charlie, Dark Horse. Just in the nick of time."

"Where do you want us, Reaper One?" the pilot asked.

"On the rooftop, Dark Horse. Just come to a hover and we'll climb aboard."

"Roger that. Dark Horse One-One inbound."

The Black Hawk came back around, and the pilot pointed its nose at the mansion's rooftop. He came in low and fast, flaring at the last minute and coming to a low hover. The door gunner opened fire, giving them cover.

Brick pushed Han forward roughly and loaded him onto the helicopter. In less than a minute, the rest were aboard, and the pilot was pulling up and away. Another successful mission.

Another kick in the teeth for Rassie Markram.

But he was about to strike back, in a big way.

CHAPTER 15

MOSEKI CAMP

Chernov deployed his men under the cover of darkness ready to attack the camp with the support of helicopter gunships. They were a mile from Moseki and holding, waiting for the squads to get into position. His intel told him that apart from the base element, two advisory teams, and a limited number from the anti-poaching squad, they had them outnumbered. According to Markram, the time was right to teach them who really ran Africa.

"All assault teams, ready. Mortar teams standby," he said in his deep voice over the radio. "Bear One and Two, attack now. I repeat, attack now."

It had begun.

———

"ALL TEAMS HAVE BEEN EXTRACTED, MA'AM," Rani said to Cara. "Won't be long and we can all go to bed."

Cara nodded. "Good, I'm damn tired."

Suddenly an alarm went off on the screen and a light started to flash. Rani frowned. "What the hell?"

She typed a couple of commands and the large screen changed to a split one. "No, no, no."

"What is that?" Cara asked.

"We've got helicopters in bound and the dots are people. Lots of them." She turned her head and looked at Cara. "We're under attack, ma'am."

It was that moment that brought the first explosion.

Cara hit the red button on the wall and the alarm started to sound across the camp. She turned back to the screen. "How did this damn well happen? Rani, tell the teams who are out what is happening. Then get yourself a weapon. You're going to need it."

"Yes, ma'am."

Cara grabbed a red phone on the desk and waited a couple of heartbeats before it was picked up. In that time, more explosions rocked the camp getting closer to their TOC.

"Name and location?" the voice on the other end asked.

"This is Cara Billings at Moseki Camp. We are under attack. I say we are under attack by a superior force."

She didn't bother waiting for a reply, just slammed down the receiver and ran and opened the gun cabinet in her office just off the TOC. Inside, she reached for her body armor and her weapon, an M6A2. Once those were in hand, she grabbed spare ammunition and her handgun. She emerged from her office and found Rani coming toward her.

The Bravo Team commander tossed her a set of NODs. "We might need these, ma'am."

Another explosion shattered the camp, followed by four more, all close together. "Rockets."

As though on cue, two helicopters blew over the camp.

They were about to leave the TOC when Luke Sayers and Henry Blake appeared. All were decked out for war. Sayers said, "We've got a shit show out there, ma'am."

Cara nodded. "We're under attack by superior numbers. Get defensive teams set up with Kayla's women under command of our people. They may know about poaching, but they know nothing about fighting a battle like this. Take what you need from the store. Go."

The two strike team leaders disappeared and Cara was about to speak when Teller, Ferrero, and Traynor appeared with Swift. "Cara, what the hell is going on?"

She gave him a quick rundown. "Can you and Slick direct things from here?"

"We can do it."

Another explosion. This one was closer still. "Teller, Traynor, gear up. Gather some of Kayla's women and dig in. I want everyone on comms."

Cara started out the door into the night. Ferrero called after her, "Be careful."

"There's no such thing tonight, Luis. Good luck."

———

THE INCOMING MORTAR rounds were hitting faster and thicker. Great gouts of earth lifted skyward. Already buildings were burning and casting an orange glow across the camp. The sound of a light machine gun reached out through the darkness and Cara realized that one of the team men had reacted swiftly and grabbed one.

"Slick, are you up yet?" Cara asked as another explosion forced her down to a knee.

"Read you, ma'am."

"Where am I needed?"

"North part of the camp. It looks like they're hitting there the hardest right now."

"Roger that."

Cara turned and ran, explosions and flames happening all around. Suddenly the sky above her seemed to be torn apart as a helicopter bore down on the camp. She threw herself behind a Land Rover as the spinning rotors went overhead.

"Fucking helicopters. Can we do something about them, Luis?"

"We have the RPGs in the store we captured last month from those poachers who thought they could use them on our teams."

"Copy." Cara sprang to her feet. "Get some reinforcements to the north section."

Bullets cut through the air from the attackers firing on the camp. As she ran, she noticed a body lying on the ground in front of her. "Oh, no."

Cara stopped and checked. It was one of Kayla's women. She was beyond help. Cara kept running until she reached the underground store, charging down the stairs two at a time and through the open door. Looking around in the orange light she saw the RPG launcher.

Reaching down, Cara picked it up and grabbed two grenades. One of Kayla's girls appeared. She didn't have a weapon.

"What are you doing?"

"I need a gun."

Cara picked up two more grenades for the launcher. "Here, follow me."

Running out of the store, the pair crossed the compound to a stone wall. "Slick, where are those damn helicopters?"

"I've got one coming in from the east, ma'am."

Cara dropped her M6 and loaded the RPG. She turned to the east and waited. "What is your name, girl?"

It seemed a strange question to ask. The young squad member said, "Nuru."

"Okay, Nuru, get one of those grenades ready. Just in case."

Nuru bent and picked it up. Cara concentrated her gaze to the east and then instantly picked the helicopter up as it came in low. Its gun opened fire, spraying the camp. Cara brought the RPG launcher up and aimed at the chopper.

She waited, rounds from the helicopter spraying all around her. Then just as it seemed she would be too late, she fired.

The rocket-propelled grenade flew straight and true, but not that true, and not that straight. Still, it exploded while making contact with the tail rotor, blowing it off and sending the helicopter into a spin before it came down hard.

"Take that, asshole," Cara crowed.

Upon impact the helicopter rolled and then burst into flames, exploding almost immediately. "Slick, where is that second helicopter? I'm on a roll."

"It's coming around to the north."

"Copy." Cara looked at Nuru and held out her hand. "Give me another one. We're not done yet."

———

On the north side of the camp, Sayers was reloading his weapon while beside him, Kayla was firing in short bursts to conserve ammunition. They were there with six other women from the anti-poaching squad. One lay wounded behind cover, being tended by Mickey Porter. "That'll do you for the moment, girl."

He reached for his weapon and started firing again. Kayla asked, "How is she?"

"She'll live," he replied and fired at a shooter switching cover.

Sayers reached for a grenade and pulled the pin. He tossed it as far as he could and when it exploded, he was satisfied to see at least one shooter go down.

Kayla reloaded and was about to fire when a helicopter came in low, weapons roaring. Soon after it swept over them it was touched by death and crashed in the bush on the other side of the camp.

"Shit, you see that?" Porter asked. "The prick shot me."

Sayers turned and saw his man sitting on the hard-packed earth holding his guts in. "The Synoprathetic suit did fuck all, Luke."

"Shit, Mickey, what the fuck have you done, old mate?"

"I'll be right, Luke. I'll be—"

Then Mickey Porter died.

"Damn it," Sayers muttered and went back to firing his weapon. Moments later the push from the north petered out and a new one from the west came with the increased fire from the mortars.

———

TRAYNOR DUCKED behind a pair of thousand-liter water drums which were rapidly emptying as he changed out a spent magazine. To his right Taja was firing at shadows coming out of the dark into the orange firelight.

Both were holding the west edge of the camp along with five other women from the anti-poaching squad.

Traynor came up and fired a short burst and then dropped back down. He hit the transmit button on his comms and said, "This is Bravo Two, I need more shooters—"

BOOM!

A mortar dropped close by followed by another two. Debris fell on Traynor as though it were raining dirt. "Christ, shit. I need more shooters over to the west. They're pushing hard here."

"On my way," Cara replied.

Taja fired well-spaced shots at the camp's attackers trying to conserve ammunition. She changed out another magazine on her M6 and slapped a fresh one home. Cara came running out of the chaos and crouched next to Traynor. "Hell of a night, Pete."

"Ain't that the truth. It's times like these you wish Reaper was here."

Cara fired twice. "Don't tell them that."

"We need to move," Traynor told her. "These drums are emptying fast. Rounds will punch right through them very soon."

Cara glanced around. "The stock yards. Take the others, Taja and I will cover you."

Traynor grabbed the others while Cara and Taja laid down covering fire. They were halfway across the open ground when the mortars came down again. This time it was like being carpet bombed.

"Get down!" Cara shouted and dove to the ground.

The earth shook violently as the high explosives fell like a monsoon, blowing craters in the hardened ground. Cara felt the thump and vibrations of the explosions travel through the ground and into her body. One landed close by and it felt as though all the air was forced from her lungs.

After what seemed like an age, the mortars stopped again. Cara came to her feet and looked about. At first, she saw nothing, then she saw the bodies. Three of them, huddled together, unmoving.

"Pete?"

Suddenly torn to run to her man's aid, her stare was broken when a round passed close to her head. She snapped around and saw the shooters coming toward the camp. "This is Bravo. I need reinforcements on the west side. We're about to be overrun. I need them now."

Cara opened fire at the shooters coming her way, but she was forced back into cover from the overwhelming fire of the superior numbers. "Fuck."

Bullets ricocheted all around her. Crouched beside Cara was Taja. "Did any of the others make it?" Cara asked.

"Two. They made the yards."

Cara looked past her and could make out the two women at the yards. At least that was something.

Movement from within the camp drew her attention and she saw Blake and Teller coming toward her with some more of Kayla's people in tow. Blake crouched down beside Cara and said, "You rang, ma'am?"

"I'm glad you're here, Henry. We need to drive these assholes back."

"Where are the others?"

"We took mortar fire. There's us and two others."

"Damn it. Let's—"

"Breakthrough! Breakthrough! We've got a break-through on the east perimeter."

Cara looked at Blake. "Who was that?"

"Bob Craig."

"Fuck." Cara looked around her. "Pull everyone back to the center of the camp. We hold them there and hope we get some support before everything fucks up good and proper."

———

FERRERO PASSED a handgun to Swift and put his in its holster. He then put on his body armor and grabbed an M6A2. All around the perimeter their people were falling back. The attackers had gained the upper hand and things looked very grim.

"Anything on that support?" Ferrero demanded.

"Nothing updated. There are a couple of heli-copters on the way to provide air support but no ETA."

"Get one," Ferrero ordered as he stared at the big screen. The multitude of red dots indicated the enemy. Blue was friendly. "Damn it to hell."

Suddenly two red dots drew his attention. They were closing in on the TOC. He hadn't seen them, now it was almost too late. Ferrero spun around as they burst in. The M6 in his hands rattled to life and 5.56 rounds smashed into them, sending them to the promised land.

"That was intense," Swift said.

"Just find out where our helicopters are."

Meanwhile it looked as though everyone was congregating around their HQ. Ferrero took a harried moment to check the men he had shot. He leaned over and found nothing in their pockets, but a tattoo on one of them was telling. Former Russian Special Forces. These were Chernov's men.

"Cara, can you hear me?"

"Copy, Luis."

"They're Chernov's men. The Russian bastard is behind this."

"Copy. Anything on our support?"

Ferrero glanced at Swift. "Ten minutes."

"Ten mikes," Ferrero repeated.

"Copy. Let's hope we can hang on for that long."

———

CHERNOV WASN'T HAPPY. He'd lost the two helicopters he'd brought along, and on top of that, his men were getting cut to pieces. He turned to his radio operator. "Kolya, order the weapons trucks in. Do it now before I lose any more men."

"Yes, sir."

Chernov had four Humvees with a mix of light and heavy machine guns fitted to them. He'd hoped not to have to use them because the two helicopters should have been sufficient. But with those gone, he'd needed to inject them into the fight.

They roared out of the darkness in line abreast, their weapons chattering like jackhammers. Chernov willed them on as they closed the distance between themselves and the camp perimeter. It was make or break time, and the Russian mercenary was damned sure he wasn't going to be the one to break.

———

"Looks like they've got battle wagons coming in," Swift growled. "Bravo One, you have incoming technicals."

"Roger. We're collapsing back on the TOC. ETA on the support?"

"Five, seven minutes. Not fast enough."

"Copy. We'll just have to fight harder."

Swift was about to respond when a mortar round hit, and everything went black.

———

"The TOC has been hit," Cara heard someone say over the comms. "We're going to need some help."

"Do what you can," Cara replied. "We've got incoming technicals."

"Sean, give him a hand. The rest of my guys online," she heard Sayers say.

They found cover wherever they could as more mortars came in ahead of the vehicular onslaught. Then out of the smoke they appeared, metal monsters roaring with violence.

Bullets hammered all around them as the machine guns kept clearing their throats. Off to her left, Cara saw one of Kayla's girls fall. Bob Craig dragged her clear, checked her, then left her because she was already dead.

Rani appeared and started reloading her weapon. She opened fire at a shooter and missed. She adjusted her aim and fired again. This time there was no mistake.

To Cara's right a Cheetah man cried out and fell backward. Keeping low, Cara crawled over to him. "Where are you hit?"

"Chest, ma'am, fucking suit stopped it."

"I need you back online."

"Be right there, ma'am."

He dragged himself back to where he could fire from and started fighting once more.

"Does anyone have grenades?" Cara shouted above the din.

Craig crawled over to her. "Never leave home without them," he said to her.

"You sound like someone I used to know."

He handed her one and pulled the pin on the one he had. Then they threw them together and dropped down, waiting for the explosion.

When it came, it was combined with the sound of one of the Humvees going up with them. The other Humvees swerved away from the exploding vehicle.

They pulled away and were lost from sight behind one of the outbuildings, the firing dying away with them. Cara looked around her and said, "I need a head count."

"On it," Sayers replied.

She turned and looked at the TOC, relieved to see Ferrero and Swift still in the land of the living. Ferrero settled down beside her. "That was close."

"Are you both okay?"

"We'll live. How are the others?"

She dropped her gaze for a moment. "We've lost some of the girls. Mickey Porter too. And Traynor to a mortar round."

"Pete?"

Traynor had been with them from the start. "I'm sorry, Luis."

"Shit."

Cara was about to say more when the Humvees appeared again. Instead, she turned and opened fire at the oncoming threat.

Suddenly the lead vehicle exploded forcing the others to swerve around it. The night was then torn apart as an MH-6 helicopter flew low overhead followed by a Black Hawk. The weapons on both birds were firing bursts at unseen targets.

Minutes later all gunfire ceased across Moseki Camp. Cara stood erect, holding the M6 against her shoulder. After a long moment she turned to Ferrero. "That's it. No fucking more. When Reaper gets back, I want those packages on my desk. That South African motherfucker is going down."

Cara looked at the TOC and realized she didn't have a desk anymore. *"Fuck!"*

CHAPTER 16

TEMBO CAMP, BOTSWANA

Both Reaper and Mamba were diverted to Tembo Camp, 20 kilometers from the battered Moseki. The rest of Bravo and the HQ element were on their way there, including the anti-poaching squad women.

Word had filtered through about Traynor and the others. Kane, Knocker, and Brick sat having a beer talking about their old friend. The man had made his mark on the team and now had joined the growing list of those lost in the line of duty. Bear, Axe, Admiral Joseph, the list went on and would grow even more before they were done.

Knocker held up his beer and said, "Life is a bitch... then you die."

"I thought it was then you married one," Brick said.

"In his case, more than one," Kane replied.

"Shut up."

"You people started without me?" Cara asked as she approached the group sitting around a fire drum.

Knocker tossed her a beer and she cracked the top. After a sip she sat down on a dead log that had been pulled up. "It's been a shitty twenty-four hours."

"Yes, it has."

"Well, it stops now," Cara replied. "We're going after everyone."

"What about the head shed?" Kane asked.

"Fuck that, no more. I've asked Luis to get together target packages on Markram and Chernov."

"So, we're going back to Cameroon?" Knocker asked.

"Yes, you are."

"I can live with that, I hope."

"I'll give you all the support I can. I've reached out to the SAS and MI6 for whatever intel they can share with us. In return not only do they want Markram and Chernov out of the way, but Onana as well. He's been sweeping through Cameroon cleansing the country of anyone who doesn't support Omossola. Without him they believe Omossola will fold."

Kane drank deeply. "Who do we take first?"

"Give me a couple of days and we'll be up on intel. As far as we know, Markram is still in Cameroon. Chernov we're not sure about. He'll be off licking his wounds somewhere. We were lucky."

Lofty Travers, Kagiso, and Kayla walked over. "Can anyone join in?"

Knocker looked at Travers. "Pull up a log."

They sat and started drinking beer as well.

"How are your people, Kayla?" Cara asked.

"They are weeping for their comrades," she replied. "But tomorrow when the sun comes up, they will go back to work because if they don't, they will think that they have brought shame on their friends."

"They fought well," Cara said. "They should be proud of themselves."

Kayla nodded. "I agree. But they do not feel that way at the moment."

Over the next hour they sat and talked, as others drifted over and joined them. The last to join was Ferrero. Kane stared at his friend. "How are you doing, Luis?"

"I hate losing people, Reaper."

"Especially one that has been with us from the start," Kane said.

"He was a good man."

"How are the packages coming along?" Cara asked him.

"Cameroon is a target rich environment. Where would you like to start?"

"Where would you recommend?"

"Organize a briefing for the morning and I'll have something for you."

"I'll do that."

Kayla was sitting next to Knocker, her head leaning on his shoulder. Her eyes glinted in the firelight. He wrapped his arm around her and brought her in closer.

Rani sat across from them beside Teller. She took a pull of her beer and stared at the ground. Teller patted her thigh. "Times like these, you pick yourself up and move on."

"It feels worse than when we lost Hyena."

"You were new then," Teller said. "You've been here long enough now to get to know people."

Kane threw his bottle into the fire. "I'm done."

"Don't want another beer, Reaper?" Knocker asked his friend.

He shook his head. "I'm good."

He picked up his M6A2. It was something they were all doing now. It was called being prepared. Cara came to her feet and said, "Wait up."

She fell in beside him. "Going my way?"

"If you're going to the shower, yeah."

Cara smiled. "I could use one."

Ten minutes later they were in the same shower, soaping each other's bodies. Once they were done, they made love and then went to bed. Kane lay there listening to a couple of hyenas in the distance. They were answered by the sounds of the Painted African wild dog.

Cara rolled over and placed her head on Kane's chest. "Promise you'll be careful when I send you and the others back in there."

"We know the risks."

"I'm beginning to have second thoughts about this, John. The decision was made in the heat of the moment."

"Someone has to do the job."

"At what cost?"

Kane sighed. "I guess that remains to be seen."

———

"Welcome to Team Reaper Assassination Squad One-Oh-One. This is our first target. David Galloway," Ferrero said as everyone in the room stared at the picture on the big screen. "Markram's right-hand. He's in command of the private army. Former Zimbabwean soldier, father was Rhodesian SAS."

"Where is he?" Kane asked.

"Douala International Airport," Ferrero replied. "That is where they have set up their base of operations. The trick is to get in and get out without causing a commotion."

"I'll do it," Knocker said. "This is my thing. In the SAS we used to do this kind of op quite often."

"You can't do it on your own," Cara said.

"It's the only way to do it. I'll pose as one of their own and be in and out before anyone knows I'm there."

"He's right," Kane replied. "He'll just need support. But to get in and out like needs to be done, it's a one-man job."

"I need to know what you are proposing, Raymond," Cara said.

It was the first time he figured that she'd used his name in a different way. A caring way because they all had history. They were more than friends. He shook his head. "Sorry, boss, but it'll be a fluid situation even when I'm on the ground."

She nodded, knowing he was right once again.

"I'm going to need identification and anything else these guys have with them."

Cara looked at Swift. The computer whiz nodded. "I can get you anything you need, Raymond."

"Call me that again and I'll take you with me," Knocker said stern faced.

"Ah, sure."

"I guess we'd better get ready."

———

DOUALA, CAMEROON

Knocker had gone into the city earlier in the day. He'd been dropped outside by a Black Hawk and had been met by an MI6 officer who went by the name of Jenny

Harris. She was based in a small apartment in the center of the city where she sheltered him until that evening.

"From what we can gather," she had explained to the Brit, "Galloway is here."

Her finger stabbed at a map of the airport. "He stays there with his men. Every now and then he flies to Yaoundé but his men are his focus. They fly in and out as advisers to the rebels. He has a weakness, however. He likes women."

"What bloke doesn't?" Knocker said.

"It may give you an opening that might prove easier than the other option."

"How so?"

"He doesn't drive himself to the houses of prostitution," Harris explained. "He always has a driver."

"White girls or Black?"

"Black. He condemns them, treats them like trash to the public but when he visits the brothels it is always the Black women he wants."

"Does he beat them?"

Harris nodded.

"Has he killed any of them?"

She nodded again.

"You can get me in?"

"Have you got all the things you need?"

This time it was Knocker who nodded.

Harris said, "Galloway is due to make a visit tomorrow night. He likes Tuesdays. Uses the same driver. Your best bet is to wait there for him and then take him out. That way you don't have to run the risk of infiltrating the airport base they're using."

Knocker nodded. "Then I guess we'll go that way. All I need now is a plan."

———

THE PLAN WAS SIMPLE. Wait for Galloway to go inside the bordello, swap himself for the driver, then kill Galloway when he returned. Seemed simple enough but the outcome remained to be seen.

Knocker set himself across the street in a beat-up Land Rover, green in color, with more holes in it than one heavily eaten away by rust.

The Brit sat there and watched the street, an untraceable Glock in his lap complete with suppressor.

Every now and then a rebel group went by as they patrolled the streets of Douala. He'd gone in clean, just in case. Nothing to tell who he was or where he came from. Nothing identifying.

Then thirty minutes after he arrived, Galloway and his driver appeared. They were in a black SUV, one of many that had been flown in on the Markram transports. Knocker watched as Galloway left the vehicle and went inside the brothel.

The driver then pulled the SUV away and parked twenty meters further along the sidewalk, situated the other side of a streetlamp so the light wouldn't shine in. Possibly so he could go to sleep.

"You fucked up, mate," Knocker said in a low voice. "If you were in my squadron, I'd cut your cock off."

The Brit gave him time to get settled and then made his move. He climbed out of the Land Rover and casually walked over to the vehicle, the Glock down at his side. Once there, Knocker tapped on the window and the man looked at him before winding it down.

He snarled at the Brit, "What the fuck do you want?"

"Just come to say hello," Knocker replied and shot him in the head.

It took a few minutes making sure everything was clear but once he was done, Knocker had the driver in the cargo bay out of sight.

Then he waited.

It was dull and boring and after days of operating the fatigue was all catching up to him. Knocker slunk down and before long he was fighting off the urge to sleep.

"Not bloody good, old chap," he admonished himself. He reached automatically into his pocket for a pill which would help him stay awake. It wasn't there. He found the hole in his pocket. "Fuck you."

He continued fighting off the urge right up to the point when he felt the door beside him open and a weapon pressed against the side of his head. "Having a nice nap?"

"Shit."

———

TEMBO CAMP

Ferrero found Cara going over the latest intelligence documents required for upcoming operations. One of them pointed to a poaching gang working in Chad hitting a large herd of elephants rumored to be the last of the big ones. Cara looked up. "I have a request from a game reserve in Chad. They want help with a band of poachers that has stepped up operations."

"Can we send people?"

"I sent a request to Mary. She is dispatching Strike Team Viper to Chad and I'm sending ten of the anti-poaching squad to meet them there. As well as support staff."

Ferrero nodded.

"So, what can I do for you?"

"We seem to have a situation. Jensen has disappeared in Douala. He went on the mission to take out the target and never came back."

"What about MI6? Weren't they there watching?"

"He told them not to. He didn't want them compromising the op."

"Stupid bastard," Cara fumed. "And they have no idea what happened to him?"

Ferrero shook his head. "Not one."

"For fuck's sake, that's all we need."

"I'll get Slick on the job," Ferrero said. "Maybe he can pick something up."

"Thank you, Luis,"

Ferrero left her office, and she went to find Kane. He was taking inventory of the team's equipment along with the other members. Looking at Cara's expression, he said, "What has he done now?"

"He's disappeared." She filled him in on what they knew. "Other than that, we know no more. I've ordered Slick to look into it."

"Damn it."

"I'll let you know when I know."

"Thanks."

———

YAOUNDÉ, CAMEROON

They shifted Knocker immediately to Yaoundé. The object of the activity was to have him put on trial and then executed to show the Western World that Omossola wouldn't tolerate outside interference.

Even though the Brit was after Galloway, Omossola saw an opportunity too good to pass up. They used one of Markram's military transports and when it touched down the man himself was there to meet him.

"Mr. Jensen, it is almost a pleasure," Markram said.

"Be one if you were dead," Knocker replied.

The South African shook his head. "It would pay you to be more civil when you meet with the president."

"You mean the cock who thinks he's king?"

They climbed into a black SUV. Markram sat in the front while Knocker was in the back with two armed mercenaries for company.

They drove through Yaoundé. Despite it only being the second biggest city behind Douala, it was Cameroon's capital. The city center was home to government offices, hotels, and the central market.

However, the presidential palace was located just to the north of Yaoundé in the Etoudi district. This was where they were bound.

The building was quite impressive. It was square in shape with pointed arches around all sides. It was surrounded by lush gardens and had a paved driveway as well as multiple fountains.

The SUV pulled up at the front of the grandeur, and Knocker was escorted inside. He was shown through to a large office where Omossola awaited him.

The man looked every bit like his photos, except in those he wore jungle fatigues. Here, in the palace he was wearing a white uniform like that of a sailor. Pinned to the man's chest were rows of medal ribbons.

Knocker nodded at them. "You steal those from some dead sucker?"

"Speak only when you are told to," a voice snapped.

Knocker's stare drifted to his right where Moumi Onana stood. "I heard you were up the bush killing women and children."

"You have a big mouth."

The Brit nodded. "Yeah, gets me into trouble every now and then."

"Mr. Jensen, you will be put to death the day after tomorrow."

"What, no trial?" Knocker asked.

"We had it in your absence. You were found guilty of course—"

"Of course."

"And you will be shot alongside three other men. Traitors to our country."

"I thought I'd be special and get my own show," Knocker complained.

Omossola turned to Markram. "How are things with you, my friend?"

"Now that the mines are producing, I am faring somewhat better."

"What of your friend, Chernov? I heard he had some troubles recently."

Markram nodded, staring at Knocker. "He mistakenly underestimated his adversary."

"Got his fucking ass handed to him more like it." The Brit couldn't help himself.

Omossola turned to Onana and nodded.

The big man came around behind the Brit and hit him with the butt of his handgun after taking it from his holster. Knocker grunted and dropped to his knees. "Bollocks."

Onana hit him again and the Brit went to hands and knees. The perfect position for what came next. A hard boot into Knocker's ribs drove the air from his lungs. But Onana wasn't done. He kicked Knocker twice more then spat on him. "Maybe we teach you manners before we kill you."

Knocker groaned and gave out a sound which could have been a laugh. "You'll be fucking going."

Onana kicked him again.

"Take him away," growled Omossola. "We shall see how he does in front of the firing squad."

CHAPTER 17

Swift put his head through the doorway of Cara's office and said, "You aren't going to believe this. You need to take a look."

She hurried after him and they stopped in front of a television. Omossola was giving a speech, and standing beside him was none other than Raymond Jensen. "Shit, get Reaper."

The rebel president was giving a rambling spiel about the west and how it had interfered in his country long enough. Now there would be an example made of what happens to those who disobey the country's laws. They were going to shoot him tomorrow.

"Damn it," Cara muttered. "Not on my watch."

Kane appeared. "What is happening?"

"They're going to shoot him tomorrow."

Kane stared at the screen and saw his friend tapping on his leg. For a moment Kane said nothing but then he smiled. "Let them."

Cara turned, eyes wide. "What?"

He turned away and started walking. "Let them shoot him. He deserves it."

"Where are you going?"

"I have a beer to drink."

"Damn it, Reaper."

"He'll be fine."

————

YAOUNDÉ, CAMEROON

It was to be an execution surrounded by fanfare and ceremony. Omossola read a speech which went on for twenty minutes about how his country would no longer bow to the west, about how it would be master of its own destiny. Which was why there was a handful of Russian and Chinese dignitaries in the audience outside the presidential palace.

Inside, Knocker sat under armed guard as he waited for his violent turn in the spotlight. He glanced at one of the guards and said, "You got a beer, mate?"

The guard stared at him in silence.

"Come on, mate, I'm about to get shot and you won't give me a beer."

"You will get nothing except a bullet," Onana said as he approached them. "Or in your case, several."

"You are so fucking generous."

"I thought so."

"Do you mind if I see the prisoner?"

All eyes turned to the woman in the nun's habit. "Who are you?" Onana demanded.

"I am Sister Mary."

"Why is a nun here?" Onana asked, his eyes narrowing.

"I am here to administer last rights to the prisoner before he goes to meet our Lord and Savior," Mary explained.

"Why would you bother with him?" Onana asked bitterly.

"Everyone deserves to confess their sins before they cross over. It is the difference between going to heaven and hell. Even for you. Would you like to join in?"

He waved her off dismissively. "Make it quick."

Onana walked off, and Sister Mary came close to Knocker. She placed a hand on his shoulder and said, "You look like shit."

"You need to hang onto that for when this is over," the Brit replied with a wry smile on his bruised face.

Kayla rolled her eyes. "I have a message from John."

"What is it?"

"You are going to be shot."

"Why do I get a feeling that this isn't a joke?"

———

DRESSED IN JEANS AND SUNGLASSES, Kane stood in the crowd. In his hand was a pad and pen and he was taking notes as the speech wore on. Beside him was Kagiso with a camera posing as a media photographer. Both had forged press passes. So too did Brick and Lofty. They were posing as people from the BBC.

Kane looked around at the crowd. He'd already picked out at least four security personnel in it. But he was sure that there were more. He looked up at Omossola after making another note on his pad. The man sure could ramble on.

"That man sure can ramble," Cara said through the earwig comms device in his right ear.

"I was just thinking that. Is everything in place?"

"It should be. Now we just have to hope for things to work out."

Moments later the rhetoric stopped, and the man of the hour appeared.

———

KNOCKER COULD HEAR Omossola's drone in the background and it was becoming annoying. If they were going to shoot him, then he wished they would just get it done. Then something weird happened. An old Black man appeared, hunched over, dressed in black.

He approached the prisoner and was immediately blocked by the two guards. "Who are you?"

"Henderson, undertaker," the old man croaked.

Knocker frowned. He had a hint of a British accent.

Both guards stared at each other. "What do you want?"

The man called Henderson reached into his pocket and took out a white cloth. It was cut in the shape of a square and almost the size of a man's chest. "I need to attach this to the prisoner."

"What for?"

"Have you ever seen the mess a firing squad makes when a prisoner is shot? Terrible, terrible. You would think that being soldiers they would be able to aim straight. But no. Hits in the chest, arms, head. Awful. I even had one man shot there."

One of the guards raised his eyebrows. "There?"

The old man pointed at his groin. "There."

The guard winced.

"Then I have to come along and tidy up the mess," the man continued. "At least this way, I can pin the patch to the man's chest and give them a better target to aim at. Makes my life easier. But if you don't want me to do it, not much I can do about it. I'll just have to clean—"

"Just shut up and do it," the guard growled.

The man nodded. "Thank you."

Henderson closed the gap between himself and Knocker and started to fix the white material to his clothing. As he did so, he whispered into his ear, "Don't forget to die."

When he drew back, he looked at the white square with satisfaction and said, "That will give them something big to aim at instead of your head."

"Thanks," Knocker growled. "I think."

"Not that it will matter, you will be dead," the undertaker said and gave him a wink.

"It is time to go," one of the guards said.

They stood the Brit up and started escorting him out. Henderson called after him, "Do not worry, my friend, I will be there to take care of your earthly remains."

"You make me feel all fuzzy and warm inside," Knocker replied with a lot of sarcasm.

He was escorted outside into the hot sun and past a number of rebel officers dressed in stolen uniforms. Even Onana, who was once classed as a colonel, now wore the uniform of a general.

"Halt!"

They stopped.

Onana stepped forward. "What is this ridiculous cloth?"

"The undertaker put it there," the guard replied.

The general screwed up his face in anger and tore the material away. "Such nonsense."

Onana threw it on the ground and snapped an order for them to continue. Knocker looked at the cloth and said, "I hope these pricks can shoot straight."

———

"I HOPE the firing squad choose the right target," Kane said."

"What is the problem—oh," Cara said in his ear. "The cloth isn't there."

Kane stared at his friend. "I'm starting to think this plan wasn't such a good idea."

"You are? I never thought it was a good idea from the start. What are you going to do?"

"Let it play out."

The commotion around the press grew in intensity. They tried to move forward but were held up by the guards. Kane saw Henderson up near the place picked out for the execution. A wall had been built out of wood and a mix of sand and sawdust had been spread around for the blood.

Knocker was pushed up against the wall and left standing. A soldier came up to him and asked him if he wanted a blindfold. The Brit shook his head, and the soldier went away. Next, armed men marched in and lined up. There were five of them.

Then everything was ready for the execution.

Orders were barked.

Soldiers raised their weapons.

They aimed at their target.

And then they fired.

And Kane jumped.

And Knocker fell to the ground.

A hush fell over the crowd.

Kane watched Henderson move in. He checked the body and stood up, shaking his head. From where he stood, Kane could see the blood. He didn't know if it was real or fake.

Four guards came in and picked up Knocker as the noise in the crowd started to grow again.

"Time to go," Kane said.

All of the team melted back through the crowd and then walked to the van in the car park. As they climbed in, Kane started the motor. He reversed out of the space then turned and drove around to where the ambulance was parked.

They had just finished putting Knocker in the back. Kane wound down the window and looked at the man who was about to drive it away. "Well?" Kane asked.

The man shook his head. "I don't know. There's a lot of blood. The doctor is checking him out."

"Let's get out of here. Meet you at the hangar."

A few minutes later they were on their way, Kane following the ambulance. It took a half hour, but they arrived at the hangar on a small strip outside the city. The two vehicles were driven inside and their engines shut off.

The back doors opened, and Rosana Morales climbed out, blood on her clothes. Kane suddenly grew worried. "Well?" he asked her. "Is he okay?"

She opened her mouth to speak when a familiar face peered around the rear door of the ambulance. "You let them fucking shoot me?"

"You let them fucking shoot me?" Knocker said again as the Cessna Citation flew above 6,000 feet.

"It was the only way. I knew you would have your suit on."

"Do you have any idea how much that fucking hurt? Huh? Five bloody bullets, fair in the chest. My heart went into abnormal rhythm and the doc had to fucking jump start me to get it back."

"You're still alive," Kane pointed out.

"You're still alive." His voice was childish and laced with sarcasm. "No fucking thanks to you, mate. What if one of those blokes has aimed for my head?"

Rosanna cleared her throat. Knocker's head whipped around. "What?"

"I only counted four bruises on your chest."

Kane grinned and Knocker suddenly realized what had happened. "Oh, great, one of those tosspots did aim for my head. Shit a bloody brick."

"That's what the white cloth was for," Kane pointed out.

Knocker looked at Henderson who was actually Gary Jones from Bravo Support. He'd been wearing a latex mask to give him the appearance of an old man. Knocker said, "That worked real well, didn't it? Onana ripped it off as soon as he saw it."

Jones shrugged. "The idea was sound."

Knocker's eyes narrowed. "Do you have an earwig?"

Kane nodded.

"Give it here."

Kane passed it over. The Brit put it in and said, "I can't believe you bloody went along with this."

"In my defense, I thought it was a bad idea from the start," Cara replied.

"Whose idea was it?"

"Reaper's."

"Some bloody friends you lot are. I thought that you would at least have come in shooting. But no, you let me get bloody shot."

Kane looked over at Rosanna. "Doc?"

She sighed. "In my medical opinion, he is fine."

"He sounds fine."

"I'm sure he won't die anytime soon."

"Only the good die young, huh?"

Rosanna nodded. "Our colleague will live forever, of that, I am convinced."

"The way he complains, maybe we should have left him there," Kayla said.

"We can still push him out," Brick said. "The drop from this altitude should kill him."

"Oh great. Have fun at the expense of the almost killed guy."

Rosanna stoked his hair. "Poor baby."

"What's next, anyway?" Knocker asked.

"Nothing for you," Rosanna said. "You are in for a few days' rest."

"The hell I do, I have some people to kill."

Kane shook his head. "Doctor's orders. We're going after Chernov."

"But—"

"Case closed."

TEMBO CAMP, BOTSWANA

"We now know where Chernov is," Cara said to her people. "Licking his wounds in Cape Town. I have no idea why he is there, nor do I care. At this point in time, he has a big target painted right in the middle of his fucking forehead."

Kane watched her with interest and saw that she was bitter. Why not? Everything that had happened lately had done so on her watch and cost her people and friends.

"We're sending in a kill team," Cara continued. "This is a simple mission. We go in, kill him, and get out."

"Like Galloway?" Knocker asked.

"Galloway was a fuck up."

"I tend to agree with you there."

"I'm sending Reaper and Brick. Just—"

Knocker put up his hand. "Boss, I—"

"You are not going anywhere. Your face looks like it has all kinds of shit kicked out of it. You rest."

"I can still do it."

"Stand up."

"What?"

"Stand up," Cara demanded again.

The Brit stood and she walked directly toward him. When she reached him, she hit him in the chest. No holding back, Cara gave it everything she had.

Knocker doubled over in pain, sinking to his knees. Cara stared at him, her face showing no compassion. "You damn well stay here."

Turning, she walked back to the front of the room. As she did, Rosanna helped Knocker into his seat. He looked up at the team leader and said, "I'll just stay behind, huh?"

"Good fucking idea." Her gaze sought out Kane. "I don't care how you do it, just get it done."

"Yes, ma'am."

"See Slick for intel."

The briefing broke up and Kane went over to Knocker. "You all right?"

"Who would have thought she could hit so hard?" he replied.

"Don't kid yourself, you're hurt. Take the time and get well. When we go after Markram, I want you ready."

Knocker nodded. "All right."

"How long?" Kane asked Rosana. "I need a no bull-shit assessment."

"I'd like two weeks. But I think we can scrape through with one."

Kane turned back to his friend. "Okay?"

"Hey, I'm not arguing."

"Good."

Next the Reaper went and found Cara. "Bit tough on him, weren't you?"

"He needs to learn to follow orders."

"He follows them. He just hates being out of the fight."

"He had it coming."

"He wants these guys just as much as you do," Kane pointed out. "He might have complained but he would have stayed."

Cara stared into his eyes and was about to say something when her expression softened. "Yeah, I know. I guess I did overreact."

"We've all done it."

"I'll go and have a word to him."

"You might want to give him something to do," Kane pointed out.

"He's on rest, remember?"

"What about gathering intel. He's good at it. Sees a lot of stuff others miss."

"Okay, I'll think about it. Now, get planning, I want you and Brick on the ground in Cape Town tomorrow night."

"Yes, ma'am."

CHAPTER 18

Half-naked women strolled around the large pool, with more lazing on the sun loungers beside it. Men were trying to impress them, and one Nikita Chernov was inside the mansion upstairs on the second level romping with two others in bed.

"This guy looks like he's really grieving the loss of his men," Brick said as he watched the feeds flick through from the security cameras that Swift had channeled into their van. "Who are the other guys that are there?"

"Backers, customers," Swift said. "Potential clients as well. I see three terrorist leaders, two oligarchs, and a dead man."

"What?" Kane asked.

"In the pool, floating face down."

Kane and Brick leaned in closer to the screen in front of them. Swift was right, someone was floating face down in the pool. "Looks like it got all a bit too much," Kane said.

A while later, someone finally noticed the body and it was swiftly removed from the pool by security, and the party continued as though nothing had happened.

After another hour, the sun began to set over Cape Town and the sky turned a deep red with orange gold trim. Still the party was in full swing, the alcohol flowing freely. Chernov had emerged from his room with the ladies in tow. When he came down to the ground level, he moved toward the outdoor kitchen and began throwing steaks, sausages, and burgers on the grill.

"Looks like steaks," Brick said. "Making me hungry."

"Heads up, there is company arriving," Swift said.

They watched on as three black SUVs pulled into the driveway and stopped in front of the mansion. In total, seven men alighted, but Kane was only interested in one of them. "Slick, give me a look at the guy in the center."

The picture zoomed in and focused on an Asian man in his thirties. "Who is he?"

"Give me a moment." They watched the man enter the party while they waited for Swift. "He's a Chinese diamond miner. Fang Hao."

"Now, what would Chernov be meeting with a diamond miner for?" Kane wondered aloud.

"Maybe things aren't so sweet in the Markram bed," Brick said.

"Slick, I want to know everything about our friend Fang," Kane said. "This has more twists in it than a damn Ludlum novel."

"Let me see. Fang is the chairman and president of

Fang Enterprises. He has some large diamond mines across the globe except Africa. No, wait, he has one in Sierra Leone. It looks like it is on a watchlist for blood diamonds. Also he has ties to the Chinese government. My guess is they're trying to get into Cameroon on the ground."

"That would explain why they were there for the execution. Can we get anything from inside?"

"I'll see. If I can tap into the phones, I might be able to use the handsets as microphones. Depending on where they meet."

"Do it."

They watched the security feed and saw the two men greet each other out near the pool. They then went inside and into the library. "You have got to love technology," Swift said.

"...to see you, Fang. Would you like a drink?"

"No, thank you, Nikita. It would be best to discuss business. I have to fly out in an hour."

"Fine, comrade, fine. I would offer you a diamond mine, Fang."

"What mine would that be?" Fang asked.

"The Lord Wellington in Cameroon."

Kane and Brick looked at each other. Brick nodded. "Rats in the ranks."

"I thought that was in possession of Rassie Markram."

"It is but he owes me money for which he hasn't paid."

"So you would take control of it and then offer it to me for a sum of money, of course?"

"Of course. However, you would have to deal with Omossola. Negotiate terms."

"What is to stop me from doing that anyway?"

"Because I will get rid of Markram. Once he is out of the way, then your path is clear."

"Fine. If you can deliver, then I will do the rest. The question is, how much compensation do you want?"

"Two million in diamonds."

There was a silence before Fang answered. *"I think we can agree to those terms."*

The conversation faded out. Kane looked at Brick and said, "Like I said, more twists and turns..."

"What are we going to do?" Brick asked.

"Stay with the plan. That mine belongs to a British company and if the Chinese get their hooks into it, then the Brits can kiss it goodbye. It would be good to leave Chernov to solve our problem, but if we do that, it'll create a bigger problem."

They waited until dark, by which time Fang had left, and the party had turned into a drunken orgy. Those who weren't drunk were well on the way. Kane looked at the screen and nodded. "It's time to go."

Exiting the van, the team members walked across the street to the mansion. They were dressed casually and had masks ready to go. "Slick, kill the security cameras."

"Going down, now. All clear."

They entered the grounds of the mansion by scaling the fence. Then keeping to the shadows, they approached the house. Out back around the pool, even in it, men and women were engaged in animalistic sex acts. Otherwise occupied was good.

Kane and Brick entered the house through a side door which took them through a laundry and into a hall-way. They pulled their masks down and took out their suppressed weapons. "Slick, where is he?"

"Upstairs, last room on the right. Be aware, he isn't alone. There are three others in there with him."

They went up the stairs and walked along the hallway. When they reached the target doorway, they stopped. Kane leaned in close to listen. There were noises coming from within. Sexual, erotic noises.

Kane tried the doorknob and it turned. He brought his P226 up, stepping across the threshold and then walked into the room. Brick came in close behind him and stepped to his left.

All four people were entwined on the bed, arms and legs going everywhere Chernov was on top of a blonde headed girl, his ass rising up and down like a piston. Her head was laid back as she screamed with pleasure, the two other girls were nibbling at her nipples.

Kane moved in beside the bed. All were oblivious to the presence of the interlopers. He raised the P226 and held it only a few inches from the back of Chernov's head. Then he pulled the trigger.

Before the girls could react, both men had turned and walked out of the room, their heads still covered in the masks. Screams started coming from the bedroom. "Slick, tell the boss job's done. We're getting out of here now."

"Copy, Reaper. I'll let her know. Everything looks clear for the exfil."

Four minutes later, they'd left the mansion, climbed into the van, and were driving away.

———

YAOUNDÉ, CAMEROON

"Someone killed Nikita Chernov, David," Markram said with a worried expression on his face. "I think we know who it was."

"Global mercenaries."

The diamond mine magnate nodded. "They just walked into his mansion in Cape Town and shot him in the back of his head. These people are becoming more and more of a problem. I don't know why they are bothering me. I really don't."

"Maybe it could be the poaching," Galloway reminded him.

"I wish they would mind their own business. Christ, they just won't go away."

"What do you want me to do about them?"

"Nothing. Pull everyone in and secure all assets. Maybe they will just go away. Add extra security to the mines. I want them protected at all costs. Without them we have—I have—nothing."

Galloway looked worried. Markram frowned. "What is it, David?"

"I have a feeling this isn't about to go away. We killed one of theirs and now they killed one of ours. My feeling is that they have drawn up target packages on all of us, Rassie. We are firmly in their crosshairs."

"Then it is up to you to make sure that it doesn't happen."

"I will do my best."

———

TEMBO CAMP

The picture was a welcome one to see.

"Your next target," Cara said. "Colonel, now General, Moumi Onana. The butcher of Cameroon. You're headed back to the country. Intel has him here in the north. He's cleaning out the villages up near the diamond mines and the young men are being utilized for slave labor in Markram's mines. Your mission will be two-fold. Hit the Lord Wellington, and find Onana, and kill him."

"We'll need a bigger force on the ground," Kane said. "Along with air cover."

"You'll have it. Roy and Mamba will come with you. You'll be acting under the callsign Panther. You and Roy will be One and Two. You'll be dropped in from the Co-32. Take the mine first. That should draw Onana in. Once he comes, then you kill him."

"What's the terrain like up that way?" Kane asked.

"Dry savanna, some mountains. Rugged where the mine is."

"All the good stuff then?"

"Something like that. We'll have revolving UCAVs around the clock and a QRF if we need it. Also, an AC-130 on standby."

"That's a lot of hardware. How are you going to slip this past the head shed?"

"We don't need to," Ferrero replied. "The general has ticked it off. It seems she also can only put up with so much."

Kane looked at Roberts. "We'll need a dedicated sniper."

"Ted can take care of that."

"Fine. We'll need someone who is good with explosives, too."

Knocker cleared his throat.

Cara stared at him. "You are still on the recovery list."

The Brit glanced at Kane. "You know I'm the one you need."

"Are you ready?"

"I'm ready."

Kane turned his gaze to Cara and Ferrero. "If he says he's ready..."

Cara nodded. "All right, you can have him. He was getting under my feet anyhow."

Knocker said, "Just so you know, Markram has reinforced his people around Lord Wellington Mine in the last twenty-four hours. While I was digging through intel riding a desk, I noticed the influx."

"Any more good news?" Kane asked.

"He has around sixty men on-site."

"Great."

"Onana is riding with two hundred."

Kane looked thoughtfully at the picture of the general. "We need to draw him into a fight."

"You been drinking?" Lofty asked.

"Once he's engaged, we can hit him hard with the air assets. Whittle his forces down and then go after him."

"Makes sense," Roberts agreed, rubbing his chin contemplatively. "Get him on the run."

"Slick, can you jam his transmissions once we're engaged?"

The tech nodded and said in his best Schwarzenegger accent, "If it squawks, I can kill it."

"Great."

"Okay, dismissed. You all have jobs to do. Reaper, a word."

Kane remained behind with Cara and Ferrero. "What's up?"

"You've been hopping pretty much since all this kicked off. Mission after mission, like some action novel, no down time to recuperate. We're worried that you might be starting to burn out."

"Is this because of what happened to Knocker?"

Ferrero nodded. "He screwed up because he was tired. You know, you can only push operators so far."

Kane nodded. "I won't lie, it's been tough, but we've got another one in us."

"I'm not so sure," Cara replied.

"I tell you what, I'll have a word to my people and if they are too stretched, you can replace us with one of the other strike teams."

Both of them nodded. "Fine."

Kane went and gathered all his people so he could talk to them. "The boss is worried that we might be spreading the butter on the bread a little thin. I need to know how you're all feeling. After all, we've been burning the candle at both ends for a while now."

"This has something to do with me, doesn't it?" Knocker said.

"They're worried about all of us, Ray. You were just a symptom of a possible problem."

"I'm good now," he stated.

"I know, but the rest of us might not be. I'm starting to feel it, but I still have one more run in me." His gaze steadily wandered over the others.

Brick nodded. "I can go one more."

"I'm good for one," Lofty replied.

Kane looked at Kagiso. "How about you?"

"I only just joined."

"You still get a say."

"I'm good."

"All right, one more and then we stand down for some rest. Agreed?"

They all nodded.

"Okay, let's get together with Mamba and plan the mission."

CHAPTER 19

The dust rising out of the open cut was thick. Thicker than normal because there was no breeze to carry it away. It hung over the landscape like a heavy sea fog. Kane could feel the grit in his mouth, and they were a mile away from the cavernous hole in the ground.

Beside him lay Roberts and Knocker. Each had a pair of field glasses and were taking in the scale of the mine and the targets they would most likely hit.

Knocker said, "If we do the bulldozers, excavators, trucks, that will hurt. Hit their separation plant as well. A few well-placed charges and we'll be all good."

Kane said, "The best part is we won't have to go down into the cut. All the equipment is pulled out at the end of the day."

"What about the guards with dogs?" Roberts pointed out.

"Avoid them if possible," Kane replied. "Ted can sit up here with Lofty and provide overwatch. Once

Knocker has finished with the charges, we can put them in place."

"We're not all going down there," the Brit said. "Just a few of us. Me and you two. Too many cooks spoil the broth."

"What?"

"We'll get caught."

They continued to watch the mine, and as the sun went down later in the day Knocker prepared all the explosives that would be needed. The charges were split up between the three men as they prepared. Soon the sun would be down and then they could creep into the mine.

Knocker said to the two men, "You two do the heavy equipment. I'll take the plant. Once the charges are in place we'll meet back on the perimeter."

Kane and Brick nodded, satisfied with their instructions. Then, once the sun was gone, they moved in.

———

"THIS IS PANTHER FOUR. Panther Three hold position." The voice was calm. Ted Clarke had spotted the sentry moving toward Knocker as the Brit tried to penetrate the outer perimeter. "Just hold your position there, pal."

Knocker froze and lay flat. He could hear his breathing growing louder, his heartbeat in his ears. He waited patiently for the sentry to pass. He could hear the dog panting as it walked along beside its master.

"All clear, Panther Three. Proceed."

Knocker came to his feet and moved in slowly, cautiously. Stopping in the shadow of a large truck he looked around, waiting for a few heartbeats then kept moving. When required to, he crawled under loaders or trucks. The big machinery giving him ample clearance. Until he finally reached the plant.

"Panther Four, copy?"

"Copy, Panther Three."

"Do you see that guard?"

"Roger, he's having a smoke in the shadows near the doorway."

Knocker shifted his gaze and picked up the glowing ember at the of the end of the cigarette. He brought his M6A2 forward and cradled it against his shoulder. He sighted a half inch above the glowing tip and pulled the trigger.

The suppressed crack seemed loud under the piece of heavy equipment. The guard dropped like a stone and Knocker waited to see if the shot had been heard. When no one appeared, he slid out from beneath it and then, keeping low, ran across to where the man had fallen.

Knocker grabbed him and dragged him further around into the darker part of the shadows. He moved back to the door and opened it a crack, peering inside. It was dark. The Brit pulled down his night vision goggles before slipping inside.

Meanwhile, Kane and Roberts were placing the charges on the heavy machinery. The man called Reaper placed his first one underneath the motor of a large loader. From there, he moved onto a bigger dozer and then two more trucks. He was about to move on to another one when he froze, movement catching his eye.

"Panther One, hold position. Danger close."

Kane hugged the hard gravel. The guard appeared, along with the dog he had at his side. They stopped suddenly, and the dog turned its head and looked directly at Kane. For a moment, he thought that the animal had sensed him. But then the canine looked away and started to pull at the lead, wanting to move on.

Kane let out a long breath. Relief flooded through his body. The last thing he wanted was a firefight.

From beneath the truck, he slid out on the gravel, then hunched over, he ran across to the next vehicle in line. Kane took the last of the explosives out of his bag and then placed it in position.

Meanwhile, Roberts was doing the same. Most of his explosives had been attached to trucks, although a loader had been the subject of his last charge.

With their mission complete, the two men were about to head back to the perimeter when all hell broke loose. Gunfire ripped across the mine site. It was followed by an urgent radio call from Knocker. "Contact! Contact in the mill! I'm taking heavy fire and pinned down."

Kane muttered a curse. He brought up his M6A2 and started toward the large building where the diamonds were processed from the rock. Out of the corner of his eye, he saw Roberts coming his way. He was about to speak when—

"Down, get down."

Kane fell flat to the ground as Roberts brought up his weapon and fired a long burst over the top of his prone form. The Reaper heard a howl of pain as rounds hammered into the soft flesh of a guard. The man fell to the ground, unmoving.

Rolling over, Kane came to his feet. He brought his weapon up and swept the area to see if there were anymore. Another shooter appeared and Kane stroked the trigger of his assault weapon.

5.56-millimeter rounds spewed forth and punched holes into the man's chest. The guard did a macabre dance, before falling backward, stiffening, and then dying. It was a scene not uncommon in a movie.

Kane and Roberts moved swiftly toward the mill, both men positioning themselves on either side of the door before entry. The firing on the inside grew in intensity. "Knocker, do you copy?"

"Roger. Read you Lima Charlie."

"We're coming in? Where are you?"

"Northwest side of the building. I have four shooters to my east. All are dug in like ticks on a dog's ass."

"Copy, don't shoot us."

They entered, weapons up, and NVGs pulled down. Straight away, Kane circled around to try to flank the shooters. Then a deep rumbling sound came from outside the building and Kane felt the floor beneath him begin to vibrate. Then the mill seemed to be shaking itself apart.

———

UP ON THE HIGH GROUND, Clarke cradled his L115A2 Sniper Rifle as he swept the area. Meanwhile the others were on standby to join the fight. Clarke said to Lofty and Brick, "You need to take everyone down there before the assholes can wake up and regroup. I'll try to pin—"

The rifle slammed back against his shoulder as a figure appeared in the barracks doorway. The man was only there an instant before he disappeared, a .338 Lapua round slamming into his chest.

"I'll try to keep them pinned inside until you get down there."

"You go," said Lofty to Brick. "I'll call in Goofy."

"Roger that."

"Goofy One, Goofy One, this is Panther Six, over."

"Copy, Panther Six, this is Goofy One."

"We're in the middle of a shitstorm down here. Need some assistance, over."

"Tell us where and when, Panther."

Lofty gave him the coordinates.

Far above inside the AC-130 Gunship, the coordinates were factored in. Then, "Panther Six, this is Goofy Four, can you repeat the coordinates?"

"Tell them to hurry the fuck up," Clarke grumbled. "They're squirting out the back door like a bad case of diarrhea."

Lofty repeated the coordinates.

"Negative, Six, that's danger 'too' close."

"We have guys under fire down there, Goofy. If these others get into it, they're fucked. We need you to put fire down there now."

"No can do."

"Damn it, Goofy, just do it. I'll take responsibility for what happens."

There was a pause before, "All right, Six, but this is on you."

Moments later the 105mm howitzer opened fire and the ground around the barracks and the mill erupted like an earthen volcano had exploded.

It didn't last long but had a devastating effect on the barracks and the surrounding area. When it stopped, the building was demolished, and the debris was interspersed with human remains. Yet the gunfire still sounded.

As Brick led the rest of the team into position, he said, "Knocker, what kind of time do we have on the charges?"

"Oh, I would think at least a good ten minutes."

"Son of a bitch."

———

KANE PAUSED FIRING and looked at his illuminated watch. "More like seven," he said.

"That just makes it a whole lot better," Roberts said.

"You blokes going to take long?" Knocker asked as the firing continued. Suddenly more gunfire could be heard as another group of shooters who'd escaped the carnage outside appeared. "You know, we could have just bombed the fuck out of this place to start with."

"The mission was to limit the damage to certain infrastructure," Kane replied, firing at the intruders.

"Guess what, Reaper, it didn't work."

"No shit."

Knocker crouched behind a control panel which had more holes in it than a fishing net. More bullets punched into its soft metal skin sounding like a musician beating on a kettledrum.

Knocker reloaded his M6 with a fresh magazine and checked his watch. "Five minutes, Reaper."

He opened fire then saw a shooter fall, changing targets as the fallen man was dragged back into cover but missed. Knocker pulled back and said, "If you guys can lay down some cover, I might be able to pick up my skirts and run away."

"Have you planted the charge?"

Knocker looked down at it. "I'm sitting on top of the bastard."

"Good place to be if it goes bang. Hang on, Fanny Adams."

The incoming toward the shooters increased as Kane and Roberts sprayed them with automatic fire. It was time.

Knocker turned and ran.

Bullets chased him.

Please do not get shot.

He dived in beside Kane.

"You're still in one piece."

"I try." He looked at his watch. "Three minutes."

"Time to go."

Roberts covered them while they leapfrogged back toward the door as they took fire from two sides. Before he moved, the Mamba team leader threw smoke to cover his flank. Once that was deployed, he moved to join the others.

They covered him as he crossed to the new position. He crouched down and said, "We should be able to make the door from here."

Then things went from bad to worse when another group of Markram's mercenaries joined the fray.

———

BRICK CROUCHED DOWN and looked at his watch. "Two minutes."

Ollie Smith said, "They're cutting it fine."

To their left, the barracks burned, orange flames leaping high into the air. To their right, the survivors from the air strike were now grouped and fighting back. Incoming rounds from a light machine gun had them pinned down.

"Ted, can you get a line on that gun?" Brick asked.

Up in the ridge Clarke searched for the machine gun. He swept the ground until locating the machine gunner crouched down behind his weapon. He lined the crosshairs up on the shooter, adjusted for fall, and squeezed the trigger.

The weapon went silent.

"You're clear, Brick."

"Copy." He looked at his watch. "One minute."

"Let's go."

Ollie Smith reached out and grabbed his shoulder. "Hold it, mate. We're too late. We need to get out of here...now."

"Our friends are in there."

"That's right, and we're out here."

"Reaper, sitrep."

"We're pinned down, Brick. Take the others and get yourselves clear."

"Reaper—"

"Go."

Brick shook his head. "Fuck it. Everyone, pull back."

———

TEMBO CAMP

They had all been watching and listening to the radio traffic. Cara and Ferrero had remained silent, choosing to let their people work the problem. Even when Lofty had called in the danger close air strike they chose to remain silent.

Now they had one team pinned down inside the mill, the others were pulling back, and the countdown was a minute to midnight.

"Ma'am, what do you want me to do?" Rani asked as she stared at her screen.

"Say a prayer." Her answer was succinct. "There is nothing we can do. It's in God's hands."

"I calculate there is about thirty seconds to go."

Cara stared at the screen.

She counted down in her mind.

She blinked.

Everything exploded.

————

How THEY SURVIVED the blast they didn't know. The explosion wrecked the mill and crashed debris down all around them. When everything had stopped, Kane said, "Knocker, Roy?"

"Here," Roberts replied.

"Great," said Knocker. "I fucking die and I still can't get away from you."

"You're not dead, idiot."

"I feel like I should be. First, I get shot by a bloody firing squad, and now I get blown up. Bollocks."

Kane came to his feet and looked around. Fires had started and would soon take hold. "We need to get out of here."

He helped the others up. Between them they had a few cuts but mostly contusions. They limped outside and surveyed the carnage. Trucks and machinery burned. The barracks were gone, and craters dotted the area surrounding them. Kane said, "I guess we accomplished what we set out to. Let's get out of here before someone kills us."

When they returned to their camp, their companions were surprised to see them alive, let alone on their feet.

"How the hell did you survive that?" Brick asked as he started examining them. He broke out his bandages and creams and went to work.

"We were just lucky," Kane said. "Our comms are down."

"I'll let them know back at base," Kagiso said.

"Get ready to move."

———

TEMBO CAMP

"They're still alive," Rani said, the excitement in her voice evident.

Cara felt a surge of relief wash over her. "All of them?"

"Yes."

"Any injuries?"

"Nothing bad. Cuts and contusions."

"What are they doing now?" Cara asked.

"They're moving to their base camp. Over by Mission Ridge."

Mission Ridge was so named from the days when missionaries had worked there trying to convert the "savages" to Christianity. Now it was a shell made of rocks sourced from the surrounding area.

"Have them call in once they have arrived," Cara said.

"Yes, ma'am."

"Panther Four, copy?"

"Copy, Bravo One."

"Bravo wants you to call in once you've reached base camp, over."

"Roger that. Will pass on the message."

"Thank you. Out."

Cara turned to Ferrero. "Where are we at with Onana?"

"Last report has him and his force ten kilometers northwest of the mine. He'd burned a village and slaughtered most of the occupants. The man is an animal that needs to be culled."

"That's the plan. Now that the first part of the operation is complete, I want round the clock surveillance on Onana and his force."

"I'll have Rani draw up a rotation."

"Thank you, Luis."

"Once again, we stretch our luck thin, Cara."

She nodded. "Too thin."

———

NORTHERN CAMEROON

When the sun rose the following morning, it painted an already orange landscape luminescent. The team were an hour from base camp and hiking single file through rugged country.

Not long after dawn they were being shadowed by a lion pride. Soon after discovering the pride, they angled away from them toward a herd of zebras.

A low rumble off to their right drew their attention to a lone bull elephant with long tusks. Kagiso stopped and admired the large beast. Kane stopped beside her. "That is a magnificent animal."

"Yes, he is," Kane agreed.

"He will be lucky to see next year."

Kane knew she was right. Anywhere else and his life was uncertain. Here in Cameroon, with all that was going on, the bull was living on borrowed time. "Maybe we can do something about it."

Kagiso smiled, showing white teeth. "It is a good thought, but a foolhardy one."

They continued walking until they saw the ruins where they were to construct their base camp. As they approached, an antelope bounded away into the bush.

The team set up everything they needed, and Kane found Flint from Mamba who was their radio man. "Get me Bravo on the line, Simon."

"On it, Reaper."

Kane sat down on a rock, looking at the surrounding landscape. It was a magnificent country; such a shame it was torn apart by war.

"I've got Bravo One on the horn, Reaper."

"Thanks. Bravo One, copy?"

"Good to hear your voice, Panther One. Things looked a bit touch and go last night."

"Yeah, a bit hairy," he agreed. "We're at base camp and about to settle in for a few hours' rest. Any update on Onana?"

"Last report has his forces moving on the mine. I'll let you know if things change. Get some rest, One."

"Roger that. Out."

Kane suddenly felt exhaustion overwhelm him. He found a stone wall, sat down with his back against it, and let his head fall to his chest. Roberts had set up an OP and Bravo had eyes in the air. He was just about asleep when Knocker sat down beside him. Kane said, "If you start jabbering, I'll finish what you started at the mine."

"Nope, I'm just looking for a place to rest my head just like you."

Knocker closed his eyes. "Man, I ache."

"Getting blown up will do that."

"Yes, it will," the Brit replied in a hushed voice and not long after, they were both asleep.

———

IT WAS late afternoon when the first report came in from Tembo Camp. Roberts was sitting on the radio while the others were resting. "Panther, this is Bravo, copy?"

"Panther Two copies," Roberts said.

"Panther Two, just an update on the target. Person of interest and his force are at the mine. He has deployed a small force of scouts headed in your direction. Number is ten bodies. Expect they will reach your post just after sundown."

"Roger that. Will let One know. Panther out."

He went and found Kane who was still seated next to Knocker. Both men cradled their weapons, but their eyes were still closed. Roberts crouched down in front of them and said, "Reaper?"

Kane's eyes snapped open. "Yeah?"

"We've got a group of rebel scouts headed our way."

"Tell them to come back later," Knocker said without opening his eyes.

"How many?" Kane asked.

"Ten."

"Just a patrol. What about the others?"

"They're back at the mine."

Kane thought for a moment. "Two choices. We either move or we set up an ambush."

"I vote ambush," Knocker replied.

Roberts nodded. "Sure, but I'll bite. Why not just move?"

Kane said, "If you had to defend this place what would you do?"

"Set up on the ridge. Command the high ground."

"Exactly. Onana has more men, but we command the high ground. We take his patrol, draw him in, and use our superior firepower to defeat the enemy."

"Let's get to it then."

———

Five hundred meters from the base camp they set the ambush along the trail. They were spaced out every five meters.

Each operator settled in with NVGs on and waited for the murdering rebel scouts. An hour after the sun disappeared, the first signs of movement were detected along the trail. Clarke had set up on some high ground where he could see them coming well before anyone else.

All the team were using suppressed weapons.

"I have movement about two hundred meters out," Clarke said as he watched through his night vision binoculars.

He watched them come and changed over to his sniper rifle. "Stand by."

Kane crouched low and watched as the scouts came in along the trail and walked into the trap. The signal to open fire was when Kane took the first shot. He waited until the head of the column was level with his position and the laser sight was touching the rebel's temple.

Then he stroked the trigger and rebels died.

The first man dropped to the rocky trail and the rest of the team opened fire. Even Clarke was on the ridge.

Suppressed gunfire cracked, filling the still night. Cries of the dying tried hard to drown it out. Then just as suddenly as it had begun, the shooting stopped, and the night went quiet.

"Everyone, check in." Kane couldn't remember hearing the rebels firing a shot but in the heat of battle things seemed to get lost.

One by one they all called in.

"Knocker, Kagiso, Brick, check the bodies."

Ten minutes later Knocker found his friend talking to Roberts. "Nothing on them except for a radio."

"Where is it?" asked Kane.

The Brit said into his comms. "Kagiso, bring us the radio."

"Roger."

She emerged from the darkness a few minutes later and held out her hand. "Here it is."

Kane took it.

"What do you want us to do with the bodies?" Knocker asked.

"Burn them."

"Copy that."

Kane then focused his attention to the radio. He switched it on and turned it up. "You there, Onana?"

Nothing but static.

"Hey, you murdering son of a bitch."

"Who is this?" The voice crackled through the static.

"Onana?"

"That is General Onana." The reply was ice cold.

"Whatever. Just letting you know your boys are dead."

"Who are you?" This time the question had a harsh edge to it.

"People call me the Reaper. You can call me your worst fucking nightmare." Then Kane smashed the radio. "Job done. Let's head back to base camp and get ready."

———

TEMBO CAMP

Cara sipped her coffee and walked over to where Rani sat at her console with Swift. "What's news?"

"It looks like Reaper got to Onana. He's on the move with almost all his men. He left a handful back at the mine. Looks like he's called in a couple of helicopters too."

"What can we support them with?"

"As you know, we have the AC-130 and a UCAV in the air. I'm about to call them back so they can refuel and be ready to help when needed."

"What about with their helicopters?"

Rani said, "We anticipated that this might happen. So we had the UCAV fitted with some of the new AA-696 Raptor Air-to-Air missiles. They should suffice."

Cara nodded. "Good thinking. Are they sticking to the trail?"

"They appear to be. Reaper had the scouts' bodies burned to try to keep the predators and scavengers away."

"Fine, fine."

"Ma'am, I want permission to do a supply drop for the team?"

Cara looked at Rani thoughtfully. "How far are the rebel forces out?"

"About ninety minutes."

"How long before you can get some supplies in there?"

Rani hesitated.

"How long, Rani?"

"Thirty minutes."

Cara stared at her and then nodded. "Fine."

Rani looked relieved. "Thank you, ma'am."

"Next time, however, get permission before you dispatch it."

"Ma'am—" Rani hesitated as an incoming transmission caught her attention. After a couple of moments, she said, "Copy, Goofy, keep me updated."

"Problems?" Cara asked.

"There was an issue with the AC-130 refueling. It's been pulled away. Panther Force won't have it for cover."

"Damn it," Cara growled. "All right. Let our people on the ground know. I'll go see Luis and we'll try to organize something else."

"Yes, ma'am."

Cara hurried away to find Ferrero, meanwhile Rani delivered the bad news to her team.

CHAPTER 20

"We've got a supply drop coming in. It's twenty mikes out," Roberts told Kane.

"Do we know what's in it?"

"Claymores, extra ammo, water, rations, trip flares."

Kane nodded. "Someone is expecting us to be here a while."

"It's probably just as well. There's something else."

"There always is," Kane replied laconically.

"Goofy has been grounded. There was something wrong with the refueling. All we're going to have is the UCAV."

"Better than nothing. Get everyone together. I want to thrash a plan out before the helicopter arrives."

Ten minutes later they were all gathered. "All right, feel free to speak up if you don't agree with anything. We've lost Goofy. There is a helicopter bringing supplies in. ETA about ten minutes."

"What's on it?" Lofty asked.

"Trip flares, ammo, claymores, water, things like that."

"That answers that," Knocker said. "We're here for the duration."

Kane shook his head. "No. Quick vote. Whoever wants to head out on the helicopter, raise your hand. Majority rules, no grudges held. It's the way we roll."

No one put up their hand.

Kane was pleased. "Right, let's get down to it. We'll set up among the ruins and on the slope. I want claymores along the front. Have them rigged to be blown in two separate waves."

Knocker said, "Reaper, if they get people around behind the ridge we're screwed. What if we set up some trip flares around there and some claymores as well which can be operated from the top of the ridge."

"Who will do that?" Kane asked.

"I can," replied Clarke. "I need that high ground. I can hold it if they attack from behind until someone comes to reinforce me."

Kane nodded. "Okay. Kagiso and...who else?"

"I'll do it," Simon Flint offered.

"Fine. Take up firing positions on the slope. If the flares go off behind the ridge, don't worry about anything, just get up there and defend it."

"Yes, boss."

"Now, Lofty. Get Rhino set up. We'll probably be needing him."

"Already done."

"Ted after the chopper has gone take Simon and Kagiso and have them set out the flares and the claymores."

"Roger that."

"Where is the fallback position?" Knocker asked.

Kane pointed to a rock-strewn slope halfway up the ridge. "There."

"We're going to need an exfil route," Clarke said. "Just in case."

Kane pointed to a deep wash to their east. "There. Have claymores set up. If it happens, we blow them to make a path and hightail it that way."

"Roger that."

"Let's get to it."

They started setting up the battlefield just the way they wanted it. The helicopter, a Chinook, came in and touched down on a flat piece of ground close by. When the ramp came down Kane noticed something odd. Three armed men got off dressed in full kit. Kane recognized them straight away. It was the remaining three men from ST Cheetah.

Kane walked over to Sayers. "Good to see you, Luke. But what are you doing here?"

"Didn't think you could keep us out of the fight, did you?"

"I won't say I'm not happy you're here."

"You don't have another couple of dozen operators with you at all?"

"Sorry."

"Well, you're welcome to stay, Luke."

"We don't plan on going anywhere. Just tell us where you want us."

"Roger that."

Once the helicopter was unloaded it lifted off and then circled away to avoid going anywhere near the troops who were coming in. Once they were done, they waited.

"Panther One, this is Bravo, copy?"

It was Cara. "Copy, Bravo."

"Just a quick update, your guests have held up about two miles from your pos. My guess is that they're waiting for nightfall. Assuming that's what they're going to do, you're going to have about two hours of UCAV flight time before we need to take it off station."

"What about Goofy?"

"Not going to be back in time and the acquisition we've made are four hours away."

"Shit."

"Make preparations just in case you need them."

"Already done," Kane replied.

"Take care out there, Reaper."

"I remember once when things were a lot simpler, Cara," Kane said.

"Yes. But the bad guys are more complicated these days."

"Isn't that the truth. Reaper out."

———

ONANA GATHERED his commanders and told them what he wanted. "None of these mercenaries are to live. They are intruders in our country and should be treated as such."

"Sir, my force is ready to move out."

Onana stared at the man who had spoken. "Take them. Circle around the ridge and take the high ground beyond their camp. If you can capture that, then they will be caught like rats in a trap. Go."

The man disappeared into the darkness snapping orders, followed by forty men. The rest would be committed to a frontal assault.

Onana sat down near a fire. They would go soon.

But first there was something he had to do. Something to help the battle go his way.

Four men emerged from beyond the fire, dragging another man with them. "Who is he?" Onana asked.

"His father was a chief from the last village we attacked," one of the escorts replied. "It is said he was named after the leopard."

Onana stared at him. "Bleed him."

The young man struggled, but not for long because a razor-sharp knife opened his throat and blood flooded forth, being caught in a bowl. Then the young man was allowed to fall to the ground in an untidy heap.

The bowl was passed to Onana and he could feel the heat of the blood passing through it. He held it aloft and spoke a few words before drinking the hot, thick liquid down.

When he was done, Onana smiled, the blood had turned his teeth red, even in the orange firelight. He stood and shouted at the top of his voice, *"Go! Go my brave warriors. Bring me their heads."*

They were now ready.

———

TEMBO CAMP

"Here they come," Rani said as she watched her screen.

Beside her, Teller maneuvered the UCAV back over the base camp. "I'm going to bring it down to ten thousand. What are we seeing with the helicopters?"

"They're holding at the moment. I'd say they won't come in until the rebels are engaged."

"Are they Markram's helicopters?"

"I'm not sure." She said into her boom mic, "Panther One, copy, over?"

"Copy, Bravo One."

"Your friends are on the move."

"Roger that, we're ready for them. Out."

Rani went back to her monitor. While watching she reached for the intercom button. "Yes?"

"Ma'am, it's started."

"Okay, I'll be right over. Get everyone else in."

"Yes, ma'am."

She was about to let Ferrero know when she saw it. "Oh shit."

"What's the problem?" Teller asked.

"I've got a new contact. Someone is coming in from behind the ridge."

Teller looked at the screen and saw them. His eyes widened as he mentally counted the dots. "You have got to be kidding me. There are—"

"Another hundred at least."

"But they can't be rebels."

Rani nodded. "No, there were no others in the area. They have to be Markram's men."

Cara appeared. "Ma'am, we have a rather urgent situation developing."

She looked at the screen. "What—who are they?"

"We think they're Markram's men."

"There are so many of them."

"At least a hundred."

"How much longer can that UCAV stay on station?"

"Another hour. After that, we have to bring it in. The other isn't due for another two hours after that."

"What the hell happened with it?"

"Computer."

"Fuck."

Cara stared at the screen. There was no way she could leave her people out there without some kind of air support. "How long would it take to get an AH-64 helicopter in there?"

"Two hours."

"Order one up. In the meantime, that UCAV stays on station while it has ammunition."

"If we do that, it won't make it back."

"At this point I don't care. It stays. Let Reaper knows his night just graduated from shit to fucked up."

"Yes, ma'am."

———

MISSION RIDGE, NORTHERN CAMEROON

Galloway had handpicked the men he'd taken with him. When word had come through about the mine and then the radio message to Onana, he acted swiftly, telling Markram of his plan to take a handpicked force north to end it once and for all.

Dropped in by helicopters, they started toward the ridge where they planned to take up position and direct fire down onto the mercenaries.

With ease they moved through the darkness thanks to their NVGs. There was a small team of two operators on point, about twenty meters in front of the main force.

Galloway called a halt when they were a mile out from the ridge. He gathered his commanders and said, "Everyone remember the plan? We take the ridge with overwhelming force. If they have any sense, they will have at least one person on top. If there are more, then so be it. Jannie, take your team and push hard ahead of the main force. Take that ridge and hold it until we arrive."

"Yes, sir."

"We'll be right behind you. Now, where is the radio?"

"Sir," a thin man came forward and offered him the handpiece.

"General, can you hear me?"

"I can hear you, white man."

Galloway bit back a savage retort. "We're ready to take the ridge."

"Then you'd better hurry, we have started the attack."

"Damn him," Galloway cursed bitterly. "Jannie, move."

———

KANE SQUATTED NEXT TO KNOCKER. "Go with Kagiso and Simon. We can use the extra firepower up on the ridge now that Markram has entered the fray. Take extra ammo, and grenades. If you need more help, I'll send you someone when the time comes. Until then, hold the high ground."

"This is really starting to bring back memories."

"For me too."

"I do love this shit," the Brit growled and started up the slope.

Roberts appeared. "Everything is ready, Reaper. We're just waiting for our guests."

"This may be a stupid question, but does everyone have their Synoprathetic suits?"

"Nothing stupid about it, I've checked everyone except you."

Kane nodded. "Consider me checked."

Suddenly the night sky became brightly lit as the early warning flares were tripped. Kane brought up his M6 and said, "Luke, clack off those claymores."

———

KNOCKER WAS ALMOST to the top of the ridge when the flares went up. "I guess that's it," he grumbled.

Not long after, the approaches to the base camp exploded with orange as the claymores detonated followed by the first sporadic sounds of automatic weapons fire.

Knocker topped the rise and found the others waiting for him. "Looks like this is it. Dig in, five meters between shooters."

"You sure that's wide enough?" Ted Clarke asked.

"Probably not but I don't want us too far apart."

The sound of gunfire became louder from behind them. It was followed by grenade explosions. Flashes from gun muzzles winked chaotically from the rebel positions.

Knocker turned back and dropped his NVGs in place and stared down the slope in front of them. Approaching the base, he saw movement. "You got them, Ted?"

"Yeah. I count maybe ten. Lead element coming hard."

Knocker picked up the clacker for the first lot of claymores. He waited and when he figured the time was right, he said, "NVGs up."

They all lifted their NVGs and a few moments

later the first flare tripped, illuminating the surrounding area. Knocker gave it a few heartbeats before he clacked off the first wave of claymores. The explosions ripped along the target area and small steel balls tore through cloth and flesh.

The Brit placed the clacker down next to the second. However, he didn't pick it up. That was for when things were a lot closer. The third was a Hail Mary string. He picked up his M6 and sighted down slope. "Pick your targets, ladies and gents. And remember, Hell's Angels are watching over us."

TEMBO CAMP

"Both elements are now engaged," Rani said to Cara. "It looks like Markram's men sent a smaller force ahead to secure the ridge. They ran into a brick wall."

"What about Reaper?"

"His team is coming under heavier fire at the moment. But the claymores slowed them down."

Cara looked at the screen. She hated not being out there, but in a way, she was glad. She'd had her time under fire with the team, and it was someone else's now. "The Apache?"

"Will radio when getting close."

"UCAV?"

"Since we're not bringing it home, we're good."

A bright flash on the screen signaled another explosion. Things were gradually getting worse. Then the first casualty was reported. And things went downhill.

MISSION RIDGE BASECAMP, NORTHERN CAMEROON

Kane reloaded his M6 and sought out another target. Onana's men were pushing up hard, but they were holding. He found a shooter who was changing position, and fired in his direction. The rebel stumbled and fell.

Another group tried to push forward. Kane reached for a fragmentation grenade and pulled the pin. He threw it and shouted, "Frag out!"

The explosion followed and he heard cries from the wounded. More incoming rounds peppered his position and chips of rock stung his face. Kane muttered a curse and ducked down.

"RPG!"

The call came over the comms and it was followed by a loud explosion. Kane's ears rang and he felt a wave of heat wash over him. The firing continued but due to the ringing, it sounded a long way off.

Then came the call. "Man down! Man Down!"

"Who?" Kane snapped.

"It's Bell."

Kane realized it was Sayers, the Cheetah team leader he could hear. "Brick, check on him."

"Moving."

"Lofty, is Rhino ready to fly?"

"Just say the word, One."

"Get it up."

Lofty activated the drone and it cruised into the air. Kane heard the BRRRRRPPPPP sound of the minigun at work. Out in the orange light where the scrub was starting to burn, Kane saw a line of rebels go down like tenpins.

"Give me an update on our WIA?" the Reaper said.

"He's Cat Black, Reaper," Brick replied. "I say again. Cat Black."

Kane's face took on a grim expression. Cat Black meant the casualty was dead or dying. "Copy."

Tracer rounds lit the night sky. Some from incoming, but mostly from the AMX-4. Moments later, Lofty said, "I'm out. Need to reload."

Off to Kane's right, Roberts was holding that part of the line with Smith. They worked steadily as a team taking down rebels and watching each other's backs while they reloaded.

Roberts looked through his NVGs and cursed. "Reaper, might be time to clack off another row of claymores."

"Do it."

Moments later the detonation of the claymores could be heard.

Then the helicopters came.

CHAPTER 21

MISSION RIDGE, NORTHERN CAMEROON

They almost missed the rockets incoming. The helicopters had been flying low and had popped up to fire at the last moment. A warning shout over the net from Rani was almost too late as the helicopters fired.

Knocker hugged the rocky ground and felt the ridge shake beneath him as the four rockets thundered into it. "Fucking bollocks."

He rolled over. "Call in the ridge."

He added the last because he didn't want the comms flooded by responses from across the battlefield.

"I'm okay," Kagiso replied.

"Still alive," Clarke replied.

Nothing from Flint.

"Panther Nine, acknowledge."

Nothing.

"Four, keep sending rounds downrange. Same with you, Seven."

Knocker scooted sideways and had only gone a few

meters when the first helicopter came back. Rounds from a rotary cannon ripped across the ridge, forcing him to take cover. "Shit a brick. Bravo, I need you to do something about those bloody helicopters."

"We're working on the problem, Panther Three."

"Work faster."

The Brit lurched sideways again and found Flint. Checking him over he found a pulse but that was all. Knocker flicked on a small redlight flashlight and ran a quick check. Flint had taken a blow to the side of his head, the result of which, had knocked him out. He checked him for other wounds and broken bones. He was all clear.

Knocker slapped his face. "Hey, wake up."

Flint groaned.

"Come on, mate, wake up, time to get shot at again."

"Stop fucking slapping me, will you. My head hurts enough."

"At least you're—"

The helicopters came back and ripped the ridge once more. Rounds seemed to explode everywhere.

"Christ on a crutch," Knocker growled. "Are you going to be OK?"

"Back in the fight," Flint said, then added, "I've never been to Bosnia before."

"What?"

"Here, Bosnia. I've never been here before."

"Shit." Knocker slapped him on the shoulder. "Just keep shooting bad guys, mate. You'll be fine."

Knocker took up his place back in the firing line. "Is he okay?" Clarke inquired.

"Just a concussion, he'll be fine. Poor sod thinks he's in Bosnia."

"Is that all?"

"Bravo One, what the hell is going on with those helicopters?"

TEMBO CAMP

"Rani, where are we at?" Cara demanded.

"I'm trying to get a lock on the helicopter, ma'am. If he'll stay still long enough."

She worked the joystick and the picture on her screen moved. A moment later the helicopter appeared. "Ready to fire."

A beep. "Target lock...firing...missile away."

As soon as she had fired, Rani turned the UCAV away from the target while Teller tracked the path of the missile. Then, "Target hit."

"Well done. Now get that other bastard."

"Where is he, Pete?"

Teller gave her a heading to fly and soon enough the second helicopter appeared.

"Target lock...firing...missile away."

MISSION RIDGE BASE CAMP, NORTHERN CAMEROON

Kane looked up and saw the second helicopter go down in a ball of flames. It hit the ground and the fire seemed to spread across the landscape on impact.

He dropped out another magazine and opened fire at a group advancing on his position. He saw some of the rebels fall but others pressed forward. Then they seemed to falter and fall back.

Along the line the gunfire seemed to drop away and soon it stopped. All that remained was the sound of the wounded across the battlefield.

Kane crept along to his right until he found Roberts. "How are you looking?"

"Glad we're wearing these suits underneath," came the relieved reply. "I picked up a round. Hurt like a bitch but other than that I'm fine."

Kane slapped him on the shoulder. "Good."

Finding Lofty Kane checked to see how he was doing. The operator was in the process of landing the Rhino. "I tell you what, boss, if it wasn't for this thing, we'd be in serious trouble."

"Good thing we have it then."

"Sounds like they're still going up the ridge."

Kane hadn't noticed it before, but with his attention drawn to it he did now. The rattle of gunfire could still be heard from the ridge itself. Multiple explosions rocked the night.

"Claymores," Lofty said.

Then came the call over the comms channel.

"This is Panther Three. We need support now, we're about to be overrun."

"On my way," Kane replied. "Roy, take over."

————

THE RIDGE

Knocker clacked off the last of the claymores and called for help. They were in trouble as Markram's men laid down a base of fire with a light machine gun and tried to flank them on the right and left.

He fired at shapes moving up and suddenly the ammunition in his magazine ran dry. He dropped it out and reloaded, slapping the magazine home. Bullets from the LMG peppered the ridge and forced Knocker down. To his left Kagiso was reloading her own M6A2.

"How are you doing, girl?" Knocker asked as more rounds peppered the ridge.

"I would rather be elsewhere."

"Me too," he replied and opened fire again.

"Panther Three, this is Bravo One. Copy?"

"Copy, Bravo One. We could use some help here."

"I've got a Hellfire with your name on it. Where would you like me to place it?"

"Either flank, it doesn't matter much. Just as long as it relieves the pressure."

"Copy. I'll see what I can do."

Kane dropped down beside his friend. "Cavalry is here."

"Great, a one-man army."

"How are things?"

"Just fine, we're getting the shit shot out of us and we've got a shooter whose bell has been rung so bad he thinks he's in Bosnia."

"Sounds good."

"Keep your head down, we've got a Hellfire incoming."

Kane hunkered down and turned to Kagiso as more rounds came their way. "Embrace the suck."

"What?"

"I'll explain—"

The sound of a freight train coming in was followed by a huge explosion as the Hellfire reaped devastation through the ranks of Markram's men. The whole slope seemed as though it was on fire and figures could be seen dancing among the flames.

"That'll ruin your day," Knocker said.

"Panther Three, how are you looking there?"

"How about another run, Bravo?"

"Where do you want it?"

"The other flank."

"Hang onto your NVGs, Panther Three."

Gunfire still sounded but the quantity was much less than before. Moments later another Hellfire smashed into the opposite flank, killing the assault.

"That's it, Panther Three. Right about now we're going to find a place to crash it. We're bingo on fuel."

"How about on top of Onana's head?"

"I'll see what we can do."

Using the ISR feed, Rani put the UCAV into a turn and pointed the nose at the rebel position. It gathered speed as it went down in a steep dive and then hit. Those on the ridge almost felt the concussion wave from the impact.

"With a little luck, Bravo One, that landed right on the bastard's cranium."

"We can only hope. Let Panther One know that we now have no air assets in the area until the next one comes on station after dawn."

"Roger that."

The ridge went silent. The only thing that could be heard was the roaring of the fire in the African scrub. The wall of flames had been impassable before it started to die down. It also worked to calm the situation and provide the defenders with a break before the next go round.

Kane said, "Get ready, they'll be back."

"I hope so," the Brit growled. "I've still got some ammunition left."

———

Galloway was fuming. The last blast and the fire had taken out at least half of his remaining force. The rest had walked into the claymores. He glared at the approaching figure and said, "Well?"

"We have ten men still able to fight. Including yourself."

"We have to take that ridge if we are to beat them," Galloway growled. He leaned down and picked up a weapon. "I will lead the assault myself."

"The men need a rest, sir."

"Fine, we will go at dawn. But whatever happens, we take that ridge."

"Yes, sir."

———

The rest of the night went by in relative silence. Then as the sun broke over the horizon, bathing the landscape in red, everything changed. A brown smudge stained what should have been a beautiful sunrise. A remnant of the fires that were all but burned out. Kane was crouched down behind a stone wall eating MREs.

"I have movement below the ridge," Knocker said. "I'm guessing they're awake."

Since the loss of the UCAV Swift had tried to repurpose a satellite to no avail. Which meant they were down to the good old-fashioned art of warfare. See the enemy, kill the enemy.

"What have you got?" Kane asked.

"They're coming straight at us."

"Hold the ridge, Knocker. If they take it, then we're done."

"Roger that."

Roberts crawled in beside Kane. "Looks like a coordinated attack. Onana's boys are coming back for more."

"Then I guess we'd best say good morning." An explosion ripped the morning apart and the telltale smoke trail signaled that their weapon of choice had been an RPG. Rocks rained harmlessly down from the explosion where the grenade had fallen short. "Nope, they beat us to it."

Gunfire erupted along the entire front as the rebels seemed to come out of the ground. Kane could hear the Rhino over the din as its weapon began tearing holes in the advancing line of fighters. Lofty had been right. Without it, they would be in trouble.

More explosions, this time closer as the shooters found their range. Kane opened fire at an approaching rebel and saw him fall. Dead or wounded, it didn't matter, he was one less to worry about.

Suddenly the incoming explosions took on a different feel. They were coming more regularly. The defenders hit the ground, taking cover with their arms over their heads. "Mortars," Kane growled. "They must have brought them in from somewhere."

"Which means they possibly have reinforcements," Roberts said as another round landed close.

"They're walking them in on us," Bob Craig said over the net. "They'll be—"

BOOM!

The transmission ceased. Bob Craig had taken a direct mortar hit on his defensive position.

"Damn it," Kane snapped. "Bravo, copy?"

"Read you Lima Charlie, Panther One." It was Ferrero.

"Do you have eyes yet?"

"Negative, we're in the blind. Don't expect eyes for another thirty mikes."

"Roger that," Kane said, reloading. "Looks like we're on our own."

"Sorry, Reaper."

"Everyone, listen—"

BOOM!

"Listen up. Fall back to the ridge. Dig in on the slope."

The remaining survivors called in and began falling back up the ridge, bouncing from cover to cover.

Once they were settled in, Kane checked on each member of the team. Now they had to fight. And fight they did.

———

THE RIDGE

Knocker felt the bullet hit home and the air rushed from his lungs. He crashed onto his back and arched his spine trying to alleviate the pain, with no luck. Kagiso rushed to his side. "Are you okay?"

"I'll be fine. Keep shooting, girl."

She turned and began firing at the men leapfrogging up the slope. Knocker dragged himself up and winced. Then commenced firing again.

"Argh!"

Knocker looked to his left and saw Clarke down. He crawled over to him and found the blood instantly.

He had a head wound. How bad, Knocker didn't know, but the man was out of the fight. They were down to three.

Suddenly he caught something out of the corner of his eye sailing through the air. "Ah, bollocks. Grenade!"

He threw himself flat, covering Clarke with his body. The explosion from the fragmentation grenade buffeted him and the sound bounced off the ridge. Knocker spat dirt out of his mouth and glanced in Kagiso's direction. She was struggling to roll over. He scurried over to her and dragged her up. "Come on, girl, we're still in this."

Kagiso started firing again and after a short burst ran out of ammunition. Dropping out her magazine she reached for another.

And found nothing.

"Raymond, I am out."

Knocker reached for one of his spares. "Make the most of it. Single shots only."

Kagiso slapped it home and searched for a target.

"Panther Three, I'm out of ammo," Simon said.

"What about the crate?"

"It's gone. Fucking had the shit blown out of it."

"Fall back on me," Knocker said.

Flint appeared. Knocker glanced at him. "How's the head?"

"Fucking hurts."

"Grab the sniper rifle. Go with that."

"What happened to Ted? Is he alive?"

"I don't know."

Another grenade exploded and then another sailed through the air. However, this one didn't explode. It blew smoke that hung thick and heavy in the air.

"Get ready," said Knocker. "It's do or die time."

———

KANE FIRED until his magazine was dry then pulled the P226 from its holster and shot the closest rebel to him. The man fell back, dropping his weapon. Kane shifted his aim and shot a second rebel in the face.

To his right, Roberts had discarded his own rifle and was using his handgun. The bodies were starting to pile up on the hill and at its base.

A group of rebels started up the slope toward Ollie Smith's position. The operator had been wounded and was sluggish in all he was doing. They were almost on top of him when the Rhino appeared above and hammered them with a hundred rounds in no time. They screamed and fell to the rocky ground.

Then the small UCAV flew out further and unleashed hell on more of Onana's men until its magazine ran dry.

"Panther One, I'm done on minigun ammo."

"Roger that. It was good while it lasted."

Lofty let the machine crash and grabbed up his rifle and joined the fight.

Luke Sayers had been working methodically at killing all the rebels he could. He'd been forced to change positions a couple of times and was working on that theory again. Grabbing a grenade he pulled the pin. Then he tossed it down the slope, waiting for the explosion.

When it blew, he came up to a crouching position and ran across the slope toward another larger sized rock.

He almost made it before a round hit his boot. With a shout of pain, Sayers hit the ground and rolled.

Roberts came from behind a large rock and grabbed him, dragging him to safety.

"Thanks, Robbo," Sayers groaned. "I think I'm going to be out of action for a while."

Roberts checked his foot. It was bloody and leaking through the hole created by the bullet. "Flesh wound. You'll live."

Kane's voice came over the radio. "Everyone, heads up, they're coming again."

———

GALLOWAY'S REMAINING fighters came out of the smoke like wraiths, angry, baying for blood. Knocker discarded his empty weapon and fired at the nearest shooter with his handgun. The man staggered and fell. The Brit changed his aim and snapped a shot at another. In his haste he'd missed.

The man launched himself at Knocker, hitting him hard. The Brit staggered back, his attacker falling on top of him. Suddenly he realized who it was. "Be fucked."

"You are dead," Galloway hissed, spittle flying from his lips.

"Do I look bloody dead, dickhead?"

Knocker hit him in the face, making him roll away. Galloway launched himself to his feet and tried to bring his weapon up, but the Brit knocked it aside as he too stood erect. Knocker went to hit him again, but Galloway blocked it and counterpunched with a solid blow to the jaw.

Knocker staggered back and tripped on a rock. This time Galloway drew his handgun, a sneer parting his lips. "You will die this time, British bastard."

Suddenly Galloway's head exploded, and he fell to the ground. Standing behind him was a familiar face.

"What the fuck are you doing down there, you lazy bastard?"

"You're a bloody sight for sore eyes, Paddy," Knocker said to the Legionnaire, taking his hand.

Paddy pulled him to his feet. "Come on, we've got a battle to win."

Knocker looked down the reverse slope of the ridge and saw at least thirty Frenchmen ascending it. "What the hell are you scousers doing here?"

"Heard you guys were in trouble. The commandant made a call asking for volunteers and here we are."

Knocker pointed back over his shoulder. "You blokes got a medic?"

"Sure."

"Good, because we need one."

———

KANE THREW his handgun at the nearest rebel and followed it with himself. He brought an elbow around and smashed it into the face of the man, dropping him to his knees. Bending down, Kane picked up his weapon and as he straightened up, Onana stepped in front of him and let loose with a short burst of gunfire.

The rounds hit Kane in the torso and drove him backward. The big man felt as though he'd been kicked by a hundred horses and for a moment blacked out from the pain.

Thinking that Kane was dead, Onana turned away looking for another victim. This time he found Ollie Smith, gun in hand, grappling with one of the rebels.

Smith shoved him away and used his handgun to deadly effect, shooting the rebel in the head and chest.

Then he suffered the same fate as Kane. One of Onana's bullets, however, hit him in the head, and Ollie Smith died instantly.

Kane drew his combat knife and lurched forward, Onana's back to the man he thought was already dead. Then something made him turn. Maybe it was just a feeling that something wasn't right.

When he saw Kane, his eyes widened at what he thought was an apparition. "No! No!"

The knife came up and pierced the flesh just behind Onana's chin. The point drove upward, slicing through the man's tongue, the roof of his mouth, and punching through into his brain.

Onana went rigid, jerked a moment, and then when Kane withdrew the knife, fell stiffly to the hard ground.

The muscles of Kane's body contracted as he raised his face to the sky and let out a piercing battle cry. One which was drowned out by the roar of the Apache helicopter as it flew low over the ridge.

———

KANE WINCED as Brick wrapped bandages around his chest to support the two broken ribs he'd suffered when the bullets had impacted the Synoprathetic suit. Once again it had done its job.

"We really need something better like an exoskeleton made from body armor," Kane said.

"You are lucky to be alive," Brick replied.

Kane nodded. "Yeah."

"It is good to see you again, my friend," Commandant Theo Giroud said to Kane.

"Not as good as it is to see you."

"You lost some people, yes?"

The Reaper nodded. "Three dead, a couple wounded. Could have been a lot worse."

Giroud looked around at the battle site. "They paid dearly for it."

"We got Onana and Galloway."

"Africa will be a lot better place without them."

"There are two more left," Kane reminded him.

"They will get theirs," Giroud said.

Knocker walked up beside the Frenchman. "How are you feeling, oh great one?"

"Go on, gloat," Kane growled.

"Payback is a bitch, yes, it is." Knocker touched a bruise on his face. "I need a beer. No, I need two. I owe Paddy one."

"How is Kagiso?"

"Still in one piece. She held her own pretty well."

"What about Clarke?"

"Skull fracture. Should be right after some treatment."

"We're getting too old for this shit, Knocker."

The Brit sat down and sighed. "And yet, here we are." He lay back. "Wake me up when the heli gets here."

"Roger that."

———

TEMBO CAMP

Disembarking from the helicopter, the weary team trudged toward the barracks they had been assigned. All were dirty, dust covered, and had dried blood somewhere upon them. Their wounded had been evacuated and the dead as well. Cara watched as they approached her, a tear in her eye. She wiped it away and when Kane reached her, she said, "It is good to have you home."

"It's good to be back."

"I—I'm sorry."

"Don't be. We all knew what we were doing."

Knocker walked past them. "You need to get Rosanna to look at his busted ribs."

Cara stared at him. "Ribs?"

"Long story."

"Have a shower and go see her," Cara said.

"She'll have a lineup." He looked over at Ferrero and nodded. "Galloway is gone. So is Onana. You can cross them off your list. Just leaves—"

"Worry about that later."

Kane nodded. "Yeah."

Knocker kept walking and was met by Rani. She looked at him and took in his tired posture. "Are you all right, Raymond?"

He gave her a tired smile. "Rani, my dear, I've had a shit couple of days. Right now, a shower and a beer will hit the spot."

She fell in beside him. "I'm glad you're okay."

"You want to help an old man back to the barracks?"

"Sure," she said, putting her arm around him. "How's that?"

"Just fine, Rani, just fine. You did good."

Kayla waited for Kagiso, noting the droop of her shoulders, most likely from weariness. She said, "Straighten up. Look like the woman we are all proud of."

Kagiso gave her a tired smile but did as ordered. Kayla stepped in close and gave her a hug. "You are the lion all of us want to be. I am proud to know you, Kagiso."

"I am a tired lion, Kayla."

"Come, let's get you cleaned up and something to eat."

———

ONE WEEK LATER

Knocker lay back on the sofa with his head on Rani's lap. He was reading a book, and she was checking things on her cell phone. Kane was in a recliner with his eyes closed and a beer in his hand. The team had been ordered to rest and that was exactly what they were doing. Kayla came in and looked over at Rani and Knocker. Rani tapped his shoulder. "Hey, your new pillow is here."

Struggling to sit up, he waited while Kayla and Rani changed positions. He placed his head on her lap and went back to his book.

Next to enter the rec room was Cara. She spotted Kane and placed herself on his lap and swung her feet over. "This is highly inappropriate."

Kane grunted, then winced. "Busted ribs."

Cara leaned in and kissed him. "Poor baby."

"Hurting."

She climbed off and sat on the arm. "Our friend Rassie Markram has gone back to South Africa. It seems he thinks he's safe there."

"What about Omossola?" Knocker asked.

"Forget about him. We're not going back into Cameroon."

"I volunteer," Knocker said.

"For what?"

"You know what."

CHAPTER 22

Rassie Markram felt weary as he sat in the rear of his SUV watching the orange streetlamps flick past. He let out a long sigh and felt the SUV slow as it prepared to turn into the gated community with his mansion nestled in the heart of it.

Tires crunched on the dirt covered asphalt of his driveway and he made a mental note to have it cleaned. The SUV stopped at the base of the stairs at the top of the turnaround. The front door was guarded by two armed men. The rest of the small estate had roving patrols twenty-four hours a day and security cameras sited throughout.

The door closed behind him, and he started up the stairs. His night wasn't over. He had a small stack of files to go through to find a replacement for Galloway. Damn him for getting himself killed.

Markram said goodnight to his men and walked

through the door to the large entry hall. He looked at his watch. His wife and son would be in bed.

Markram hung his coat on the dark wooden coat rack and walked across the hallway to the door opposite. He opened it and walked inside, flicking on the desk lamp as he passed it, then walked over to the drinks cabinet on the far wall.

Pouring and extra two fingers of brandy, he stoppered the crystal decanter. When he turned, he froze. "You—you're dead."

"Galloway said that too," Knocker replied, waving the suppressed handgun toward the desk. "Sit down and enjoy your drink."

Markram followed the instructions and sat. He took a sip of his drink and Knocker did the same, having poured himself one while waiting for his target. "What have you done with my wife and son?"

"As far as I know they're still upstairs asleep."

"You are here to kill me." It was a statement.

"Nothing personal," Knocker replied. Then with a shrug he added, "Bollocks, it's bloody personal."

Markram took another sip. "I can pay you well if you leave now. Two—three million dollars? Pounds? Whatever you want. Gold? Diamonds?"

The Brit shook his head. "I have what you might call a weakness. I'm honest."

"Fuck off. You're not honest. If you were, you wouldn't be here."

Knocker nodded grimly. "You're right."

Then he shot him in the head.

———

YAOUNDÉ, CAMEROON

Fang Hao placed the glass down and stared across the desk at Ignatius Omossola. "I think we can come to an arrangement," the rebel leader said. "Soon I will be president and I will be needing investment to rebuild certain sections of my country."

Fang nodded. "We would pay you thirty percent of what comes out of the mine. But in return, my country would like something else."

"What would that be?"

"We would like access to port facilities, and the highways would need to be upgraded."

"And your country will supply such things for a fee?" Omossola stated.

Fang nodded. "You wouldn't have to worry about a thing."

"Is there anything else?"

"We would also provide security for your country against poachers."

"How would you do that?"

"We would train your army to a higher standard to enable them to counter the threat."

"What would you require for that?" Omossola asked.

"To do that my government would need to place an advisory force on the ground. Maybe a naval force to patrol the seaways against threats."

"How many would be in this advisory force?"

Fang hesitated. Then said, "Two thousand troops."

"What about ships?"

"Four patrol boats, three destroyers, and an aircraft carrier."

"An aircraft carrier?"

"Yes."

Omossola shook his head. The other ships, yes, but not the carrier."

Fang stared at him for a moment before nodding. "That would be acceptable."

The rebel president held out his hand. "It is a pleasure doing business with you, Mr. Fang."

———

ONE MONTH LATER

Kane and Knocker were watching the breaking news report on the large screen. The current headlines sweeping the globe were about China stationing a small fleet in Cameroon as well as armed soldiers under the guise of advisers to help with the poaching problem.

"What do you figure the pricks are up to?" Knocker asked.

"Fang is after the diamond mines. The Chinese will be after all the riches that country can supply. Including the naval base that we're seeing now. It would give them a second permanent presence in the southern Atlantic."

Knocker nodded. "It's going to be bad, isn't it? They're going to start running poaching operations out of Cameroon to supply their market."

"It's possible, I guess."

"And if they do, we're going to get the call. Shit, just what I always wanted, another damn war with China."

Kane was about to respond when Cara appeared. "Gear up, the team in Chad is in trouble."

Kane slapped him on the shoulder. "Looks like it has already started."

**FROM THE AUTHOR OF THE TEAM REAPER
SERIES COMES KANE.**

When John 'Reaper' Kane is forced to gun down a fourteen-
year-old boy in self-defense, the combat-weary warrior
becomes disillusioned with the endless cycle of blood and
violence his life has become.

Going off-grid in the remote mountain town of Vesper Lake
for a week of soul-searching, he steps in to help a young
woman, and his two-fisted interference finds him running
afoul of the local sheriff. In the violent aftermath, he discovers
that the town suffers under the crushing stranglehold of
Nazareno 'The Nazarene Dragon' Pedregon, a ruthless drug
lord commanding his criminal empire from inside Black Bog
Federal Prison, a cesspool of death and corruption.

Framed for murder, Kane is dragged into the prison and
forced to fight for his life when Nazareno finds out who he
really is. Alone, exhausted, and outgunned, with enemies
closing in on all sides, the odds are stacked against him. But
when the hunt turns primal, Kane knows that the only way to
survive is by tooth and nail.

AVAILABLE NOW

ABOUT THE AUTHOR

A relative newcomer to the world of writing, Brent Towns self-published his first book in 2015. *Last Stand in Sanctuary* took him two years to write. His first hard-cover book was published the following year.

Since then, he has written twenty-six Westerns, including some in collaboration with Ben Bridges; several action adventure novels; the novelization to the 2019 movie, *Bill Tilghman and the Outlaws*; as well as scripted a handful of Commando Comics. Not bad for an Australian author, he thinks.

Often up until the small hours of the night, bashing away at his tortured keyboard in Queensland, Australia, Brent loves to lose himself in the world of fiction. If you're interested in sharing your thoughts in more detail, scan the QR code below! Your feedback is invaluable to him—and often helps shape his future writing endeavors.

Made in United States
Orlando, FL
10 May 2024

46709342R00183